SP.

GROWING ANYWAY UP

GROWING ANYWAY UP

Florence Parry Heide

J. B. Lippincott Company / Philadelphia and New York

U.S. LIBRARY OF CONGRESS CATALOGING IN PUBLICATION DATA

HEIDE, FLORENCE PARRY.
   GROWING ANYWAY UP.

SUMMARY: WITH THE HELP OF HER AUNT, FLORENCE IS FINALLY ABLE TO
FACE A PROBLEM SHE HAS REPRESSED FOR YEARS AND ADJUST TO THE CHANGES
IN HER LIFE.
   I.   TITLE.
PZ7.H36GR   [FIC]   75-40033
ISBN-0-397-31657-7

TO JUDY GIRL

WITH LOVE

FROM MOM

ONE (ENO)

Maybe if I'd had a different name, things would have been better. A name like Kim, or Sascha. Or Nicole. Because the minute you're born, people start saying your name at you, and it starts making you what you are. Even when you're a little baby, you hear it about a billion times. It's practically your whole environment. So you start being it.

So you're a Florence. Listen to the nicknames. Flossie. Flo. Flop. Flop, Flopper, Floppest.

Listen to it backwards: Ecnerolf. You can tell a lot about people by their names spelled backwards.

Aunt Nina was right when she told me that time that I was a very intense person. Of course she made it sound like a compliment. If anyone else had said it, like my mother, or George, or anyone, it would have been different. My mother would have sighed one of her sighs and said, "Do you have to be so *intense*, Florence!" George would have said, "She's a very intense person." And he'd have said it to my mother, probably, when I was out of the room but could listen from my secret place. Or maybe he'd have said it even when I was right there in the room with him. He usually talks as if I'm not there or stone deaf or something. He almost never talks directly to me. Even when he does, he doesn't ever really *say* anything. It's always, "Be sure to hang up your coat," something dumb like that, because he's such a dumb person. How my mother could even stand him, let alone marry him, I don't know.

Intense. The girls at that silly Chilton school would have whispered it behind my back, but loud enough so that I'd be sure to hear it. Well, the fact is they wouldn't even have known what it meant, or how to spell it. They didn't know anything, they never will, no matter how old they get.

Miss Perkins would have looked over her glasses at me and smiled that sickly smile and said, "My, we're intense today, aren't we?" She's a very sickly person, Miss Perkins. She doesn't even have a first name. I know for a fact that she was never a little baby. She was born just a smaller version of Miss Perkins today, with her hair in a bun and those owly glasses. I christen you Miss Snikrep.

Intense. The singular of intense is inten. Backwards it is esnetni. I am a very intense person. Person, intense, very, a, am, I. A very person, intense am I. I am a very person, intense. Esnetni: Es-net-ni. Esnetni, Esnetni, you are my love.

The things I'm going to tell about happened a million years ago, before I'd even met Aunt Nina, or George, or anyone. Everything changed then, everything but my name. Even if I changed it now, it's made its mark on me, just as living in this skin has made *its* mark.

My mother and I had been living in Florida for as long as I could remember, in a little house like all the other houses, in a little town like all the other towns. Sunshine, hot, all the days the same, all flat, all going the same way.

Like those long freight trains that just go along, every car the same, who pushes? who pulls? you forget, and the reason you forget is that it doesn't matter, something or someone pushes, something or someone pulls. You're just along for the ride. That's the way it was with those days. There wasn't one day that could stand up and be counted as any different, not one day that ever swam the other direction.

That was the way we wanted it, my mother and

I, because the minute something different happened, things became very dangerous. I'd always known that, and I guess she knew it, too, because she kept everything the same, the same kinds of clothes, the same kinds of meals, the same kinds of sentences, the same kinds of thoughts. Boring, but safe, predictable. There are worse things than boring.

My mother worked in a place called the Shelle Shoppe, one of those junky gift shops for tourists. A gift shop is where you can buy something for someone else that you wouldn't want yourself, that's why they're called gift shops. And a tourist is someone who buys stuff like that, that's why they're called tourists. You've never seen so many things you wouldn't want in one place. Seashells pasted together to look like something else, something different, dumb things like that. What could be better than just plain seashells?

The minute anybody starts monkeying around with something that's perfect to begin with, then there's something wrong with that person or with the world, or maybe with me for thinking it's wrong. But how can anybody figure that seashells all pasted together and painted to look like a lady in a long dress, for instance, or a cat, or a house, could possibly be better or more interesting or more beautiful than just separate seashells that you can look at and wonder about and feel and think about?

About seashells: Inside every single one used to be a living creature. The shell was its house. Or its skin? When I was a little kid, I used to think that if I lived in the sea, I could grow a shell. I started putting salt in the tub, and I took longer and longer baths, but of course nothing happened.

Anyway, back to Ye Olde Shelle Shoppe. There were shops just like this one all up and down the street, and streets just like this one all up and down the town, and towns like this one all up and down the world. It was a place for tourists. No one else ever came in. Why would they? How could they? They'd be embarrassed.

About tourists: Tourists came to our town because they wanted to be warm or because they wanted to go to a town that wasn't their town. They never stayed long. No one ever stayed long in our town except my mother and me. The tourists all looked pretty much the same. Some were men, some were women, and all of them wore clothes they wouldn't be caught dead wearing in their own hometown, wherever that was. Anyway, they all looked the same, and what they said was all the same.

Sample tourist conversation:

CUSTOMER: Nice day, isn't it? For ducks, I mean, ha ha.

MY MOTHER: Nice and wet. But then we needed a little rain.

CUSTOMER: Rain? Rain we got, up in New Jersey. What we need is some of that good old Floriday sunnyshine.

I knew someone must have written it all out for them, and everyone must have learned their lines before they walked in. There were different sayings for different kinds of weather—rainy day, sunny hot day, sunny cool day. There were about ten scripts. Maybe my mother had written them, I don't know. She knew all the parts, anyway, and if a tourist had ever forgotten his lines, she would have prompted him.

When she wasn't talking to the customers about the weather, my mother was talking to the ladies who made the junk out of seashells and yarn and paint and pipe cleaners. "The turtles are going very well, I'll take four dozen," my mother would say. A turtle was an arrangement of seashells fixed up to look like a turtle, you guessed it, with a head that bobbed up and down. She sells seashells down by the seashore. Seashells she sells by the seashore down.

When she wasn't working at the Shoppe and I wasn't at school, we'd go to the beach. It wasn't far from our house and it was my favorite place. I'd watch the waves and listen to them and pretend that each one that broke was me. And I liked to make sand castles with moats, and I, Princess Sascha, lived in them. I'd write my name and other names and secret thoughts on the sand and watch them wash away, and I know they were being carried off in the water to another shore for someone else to find.

That sounds pretty babyish, I know. Remember I was lots younger then. But to tell the truth, if I ever get back to the ocean again, and a beach, that's exactly what I'll do.

Things had been going along like that, with every day like every other day, forever. Not for forever—there was something before this, something bad, that I'd forgotten. It was important not to remember it, and it was washed out of me like my name washed out of the sand.

And then one night my mother and I were sitting and watching some program on TV and having a TV dinner the way we usually did, and my mother said, "We're going to be moving. We're going to move up north."

Just like that. Move up north. How far is north, how high is up? Where, when, how, why?

The answers were slow in coming, because we only talked at the commercials. All of our conversations were just commercial length, whether we were watching TV or not. It was always hard for me to talk to my mother, or to anybody, even if I'd had anything to say. Question and answer, and only questions that have answers. Real questions therefore cannot be asked.

Quiz Game

Subject: Moving

Where—to someplace I'd never even heard of. Lattmore, Pennsylvania.

When—pretty soon. Right away, really. Don't worry, it's going to be all right.

How—a truck would take the furniture, she and I would drive. Drive! I hated driving trips. Getting into a box on wheels and being taken somewhere like a sack of potatoes was my idea of nothing.

Why—why, why move, why leave? Just because. Just because!

I thought maybe she'd say more about it when the program was over, but she wanted to watch the next program, too.

Did my mother watch TV the way I was watching, seeing but not seeing, listening but not listening, the inner eye and ear tuned to a different program altogether?

What about school? There was a very nice school there, a private school, all the arrangements had been made.

That's one of the things, just one, that I hate most about grown-ups, especially mothers. They go right ahead planning your life, making you change it, and you don't have anything to say about it at all. They act as if you're not a real person until you're about a million years old.

And what was this about a private school? What's a private school? An expensive school? A club? A school for private people?

She said it was a girls' school, very small, very good, very nice girls, I'd be making lots of friends, I'd like it very much. It was called Chilton Hall, and right away I knew it would be a big bleak building with chilly halls and chilly rooms, chilly corridors with rows of doors marked Private, Private—keep out, no public people allowed, and a barbed wire fence to keep public people out and keep the private people in.

What was our house going to be like? And she said, "We'll have an apartment."

An apartment! A little box inside a big box, the rooms smaller boxes inside that, and the closets smaller boxes inside those.

"How far is it from the beach?" I asked. That shows how good my geography is.

"Pennsyl*van*ia," my mother said, sighing. "There isn't any beach in Pennsylvania."

My mother sighs a lot.

About sighs: A sigh is just deep breathing.

Breathing: Out goes the bad air, in comes the good air, that's what they taught us at that dumb lifesaving class my mother had made me take the year before. Artificial respiration. So maybe my mother's sighs were saving her life. If I had looked at it that way, maybe I wouldn't have minded her sighing so much. I always suspected that the reason she sighed a lot was because she'd had me instead of one of those palsy-walsy daughters, or maybe because she knew she'd made a mistake, naming me Florence.

Anyway, we were going away. Moving.

Well, I couldn't leave. I didn't want any changes. I'd made everything here safe, but it had taken a long time. I didn't know about the next place.

If I looked to the left as far as I could without moving my head, and then to the right, and then up, and then down, it would be all right. Left, right, up, down, then around. If I did it ten times, we wouldn't move. I did it twenty to be on the safe side.

I had to be sure my mother didn't notice. She'd have been pretty upset if she thought I was doing my eyes again.

When the program was over, she said, "It's going to be fine. You'll like it, you'll see."

I said the last sentence over to myself backwards. See you'll it like you'll. "Oh, sure," I said. Sure, oh.

I had to make doubly sure I was safe that night. Look up at the four corners of the ceiling. One, two, three, four. Now the four corners of the floor. Four, three, two, one. I never could have a bed or a desk or a chair in a corner—it would have meant lifting it out each night.

Then the four corners of the window, then the closet door, then the door to my room (or to the hall, depending on whether you were in my room going into the hall or in the hall coming into my room). Tap both doors four times. Then into bed and touch the four corners of the bed. Turn the light on and off four times. Say good night four times.

Ceiling, floor, window, door
look four, tap four
bed four, light four
and now say good night four.

It didn't work. It always had, before. I was so used to doing it I never even thought about it anymore. Maybe I'd forgotten something. I turned the light on and started all over again. No good. Maybe if I did the whole thing four times it would be all right. I tried. No good.

It had to be four something. Maybe four times four. I hoped it wouldn't have to be four hundred.

I never did get that room safe again. So I was glad after all when we left.

It wasn't all that hard to leave, because we didn't have all that much stuff. I told some of the kids at school I was moving, and they didn't even ask for my new address. The only person that seemed sorry

was the lady next door, because she was afraid someone would move in that had little kids or dogs.

So we drove up north, from hot blue to cold gray.
Up from palm trees to trees with bare bones. I sat
and stared out the car window and did my eyes a
lot.

My mother doesn't like to talk when she's driving.
When we were at home, we'd talked only during
commercials. Now we talked only at stoplights or
gas stations. And of course all the motels we stopped
at had TV in the rooms: more commercials.

Why were we moving? Maybe I said it out loud,
or maybe my mother read my mind, because suddenly, at a stoplight, she said, "There wasn't anybody to say good-bye to."

It took me a minute to say it backwards to myself.
Then I asked, "Is there going to be anybody to say
hello to when we get there?"

"Of course," said my mother in a minute. "Nina.
Aunt Nina. She'll be back in Lattmore pretty soon."

I waited until we stopped for lunch before I asked
anything more. Then I said, "Who's Aunt Nina?"

My mother was quiet for so long I looked over at
her. Usually we don't look at each other when we
talk, or at all. She was frowning and looking at me.
As soon as I looked at her, she looked away.

Aunt Nina. Who was she?

My mother finally said, "You don't remember

Aunt Nina." I couldn't tell whether she was glad or disappointed. It's always hard to tell with my mother.

"Tell me," I said, looking at the menu. I always had a hamburger, but looking at the menu gave me somewhere to put my eyes.

My mother ordered us both a hamburger and french fries and a glass of milk.

"Nina is your father's sister," she finally said. "You knew her very well. You *loved* her. That was long ago. I've talked about her many times."

The fact is, I didn't remember my mother's ever talking about her. She didn't even talk about my father. He'd died when I was a little kid, that's all I knew. There had always been a picture of him on the dressing table in my mother's room, but I'd seen it too much to see it. I didn't know what he looked like any more than I knew what I looked like, or my mother.

Nina. Aunt Nina. I didn't know yet whether it was a good sound or a bad sound. Nina. Anin. Good. "What's her last name?" I asked.

"Why, it's Stirkel, same as ours," said my mother. "She's not married."

The fact that she said "She's not married," instead of "She never married," meant that my mother thought that Aunt Nina was still thinking about it. Or that my mother was still thinking about it. Or that my mother was still thinking that Aunt Nina *should be* thinking about it. Or maybe it didn't mean anything.

But whenever she talked about herself, she'd say, "I never married again."

My father's name had been James. James Stirkel. He married my mother, whose name was Elizabeth Marshall. She'd have had to like him a lot to trade a good name like Marshall for one like Stirkel. Lekrits.

Elizabeth. Now there's a nice name. You don't even have to *care* how it is backwards (Htebazile). It's got such good nicknames. Beth, Liz, Liza, Lizabee; however you do it, it's all right. It's just like my mother, though, to want to be called Elizabeth.

James and Elizabeth. They'd taken some kind of trip abroad right after they were married and had gone to Florence, Italy. That's why they called me Florence. I guess I should be glad they didn't go to Niagara Falls.

I got some more facts out of my mother, a few at a time. She hadn't seen Aunt Nina for ages. Aunt Nina had been living somewhere else, somewhere in California, for a long time, but now she lived in Lattmore. She had found an apartment for us and a job for my mother and a school for me.

I couldn't tell whether my mother was happy or excited or bored or worried about our moving to

Lattmore. She had that kind of face and that kind of voice and that kind of personality. She was that kind of person. Is.

I kept on doing my eyes the whole trip. Most of the time I was looking out the window. Eyes left, eyes right, eyes up, eyes down. Four times four and then around. And the whole time I was worrying about exercising my eyes too much. Maybe they'd fall out on my lap or fall backwards into my brain. But I had to keep doing it. If I stopped, I didn't know what would happen. Maybe I'd die, or maybe the world would come to an end. There was no way of knowing, so I had to keep doing my eyes. It felt familiar, it was as if I'd started sucking my thumb again.

If I'd been going to change my name, that would have been the time to do it. Where we were going, only my mother knew my name was Florence. My mother and Aunt Nina. But I never think of things until it's too late. So I arrived in Lattmore, Pennsylvania, as a Florence Stirkel instead of a Kim Nightingale.

TWO (OWT)

Lattmore wasn't a town at all, it was a suburb. At least, that's what my mother said as we drove in. I never have figured out the difference, unless it's that in a town you know the names of the mailmen and the milkman and the men who pick up the trash, and in a suburb you don't.

I wondered whether suburbs had newspapers.

FLORENCE STIRKEL MOVES TO LATTMORE

Today Florence Stirkel and her mother, who accompanies Miss Stirkel on her travels, arrived at their fashionable new home in Lattmore, Pennsylvania. Tastefully attired in simple blue jeans and wearing neither jewelry nor makeup, Miss Stirkel confided to this reporter that apartment living was going to be a novel experience for her. Miss Stirkel and her mother will stay at the Haven Motel while awaiting the delivery of their furniture. Miss Stirkel's aunt, Miss Nina Stirkel, plans to return to Lattmore from Europe in a few weeks.

About the apartment building: Ugly. Actually, I never notice things, according to my mother, and I guess it's true. If I had to sit down now and draw it, or describe it, I couldn't. I can't remember anything about it on the outside except the windows, because they were eyes that were watching me. Insides are different, I remember insides.

About our apartment: Big and empty and gloomy. My mother said it looked big and empty because our furniture hadn't been moved in and gloomy because it was a gloomy day, but I could tell she was having second thoughts about how it was going to be, living in a second-floor barn.

You had to walk up fifteen steps to get to the apartment. And of course down fifteen steps to get away from it, which you wanted to do right away. The trouble with being on the second floor is that every time you want to go outside, you have to think about it instead of just going. Well, what was there to go outside for, anyway? I didn't know anyone, there wasn't anywhere to go, there wasn't anything to do. I wasn't all that excited about going downstairs (fifteen) and outside just to stand on some sidewalk like a doorman. Right away I'd have to figure out the ways I could make it all safe. I could make the furniture safe, one piece at a time, when it was moved in later that week. Meantime, I could wander around the empty apartment and make every inch of it one hundred percent.

My mother never looked at me very much, but I could tell that she glanced at me two or three times while we were looking over the apartment that first day. Maybe she'd noticed that I was doing my eyes. I'd have to be more careful.

The rooms were big, and the ceilings were high, and all of it was painted a sick green. There was a living room, and a separate dining room, and a long narrow kitchen with a breakfast nook with built-in benches for people who liked to sit bolt upright every single second. My mother and I would each have a bedroom, and the bathroom was across the hall from my room.

My room was a funny shape. It had an alcove with a big window in it. That meant there were more than four corners. There were six. *That* meant a lot of figuring to make it safe. The window looked right into a window next door. I pulled the shade down. I'd have to work out a way to make my window safe and the window across from me extra safe.

My closet was like a long narrow tunnel. When I walked into it, I knew I'd have to count it as a room and do its corners every night.

"You'll have lots of room for your things," said my mother, looking around my room and peering into the closet. What things? I'd brought some books and some clothes and some notebooks. Oh, and an old doll, just because I hadn't had a chance to throw it away or anything when we moved. Of course, I hadn't played with dolls for ages. I'd stick it away in the closet.

Later I'd move my chair in there, way at the back, and listen. But that was later.

We arrived in January, right in the middle of the school year, and of course I was supposed to start school the day I got to town, but I talked my mother into letting me wait until the furniture had come and we were all settled. So things could have been worse. I did every single chair, table, bed, dresser, couch, carpet, and box—once when they were being carried up the stairs and another time after they were in the apartment.

So I had made the place as safe as I could make it. Now for the school.

The first and best thing about it was that I could walk back and forth. No bus, no car: good. My mother said that was one reason Aunt Nina had chosen this apartment. Because it was so close to the school. I could walk. The exercise would do me good, my mother told me.

Chilton Hall was one of those girls' schools where everyone but you had gone since they were born. They'd all known each other a million years. In the big Florida school I'd always gone to before, there was so much coming and going you hardly had a chance to get to know anyone's name. Everyone had been a stranger, so it didn't matter if you were one, too. Here I was the only stranger. Strange, stranger, strangest.

The outside of the school was big and bleak, just as I'd known it would be from its name, but it had lots of trees and all, and grass. The building was pretty old, and there was a big ugly new gymnasium that everyone kept talking about as if it was a new baby. I'd figure out a way to get out of gym classes, I always had. All those bodies, all that jumping around. Talk about public! Talk about private!

This Miss Perkins that I talked about before took me around and introduced me. Introduced me to everybody in the whole school. She had the same speech for every classroom. Inside of her was an old record player, and there was only this one record left: "Now, girls, here's our new girl, Florence Stirkel. We're going to make her feel right at home, aren't we? Florence is the niece of one of our old girls, and she's come all the way from Florida just to be here with us at Chilton Hall. We're all going to love having Florence become one of our Chilton girls. Let's all say, 'How do you do, Florence Stirkel.' "

All the girls were dressed the same: dark green jumpers and light green shirts or blouses. They all wore loafers. They all had long hair. And they all had the same expression, which was no expression at all. They smiled while she was talking, but you could tell they were bored. And then this chorus each time of "How do you do, Florence Stirkel." It was like a big echo chamber and hall of mirrors all rolled into one. I knew their brains were all in uniform, too. They'd all have the same thoughts, they'd all say the same things.

FLORENCE STIRKEL JOINS CHILTON ARMY

Well, I'd never look like them. Even if I had to cut my hair.

We finally got to the class I was supposed to be in. There were only fifteen girls. Miss Perkins introduced me to the history teacher, Mrs. Bolton. It was history class, but they weren't learning any history, you bet. They were all thinking about their hair. Even Mrs. Bolton kept reaching up to tuck in stray wisps of hair. And we had the records again, first Miss Perkins, then the girls. "How do you do, Florence Stirkel?" Stirkel Florence, do you do how?

FLORENCE STIRKEL ADMITS ROLE AS SPY

Cleverly disguised as a student at a select school for girls, Florence Stirkel, using one of her many aliases, was able to gather information proving that the school harbored a ring of imposters. Her testimony against a "Miss Perkins" assures the latter's conviction as ringleader of the gang.

Florence Stirkel revealed today that the students were robots dressed up to look like real people. Asked how she had discovered the deception, Miss Stirkel replied, "It's part of my job to know when people who pretend they're people aren't really people at all."

That first day I learned a lot. I learned that I wasn't going to learn a thing there. In my class they were learning things I'd known for years.

ENGLISH:	This is a sentence. Is this a question?
LATIN:	All Gaul is divided into three parts.
MATH:	Let X represent—
HISTORY:	The Revolutionary War was fought for the following reasons:

COMPOSITION: Write a three-page paper on one of
the following subjects:
My Family
The Best Time I Ever Had
Problems I Have Solved
My Favorite Vacation
My Hobby

Can you believe it?

The teachers at Chilton Hall were like the tourists in Florida: they came in different shapes, sizes, and colors (soft-round-dark, tall-thin-pale, etc.), and they all sounded alike, as if they were talking to small children who were very stupid, very sick, or very rich.

We're going to try to do our very best today, aren't we? Now, class, we're all going to pay attention to today's lesson.

Sticky sweet, cloying as molasses. You heard, but there was no way to listen. It was background music for whatever you were thinking, that's all.

The *we* thing, instead of the *you, Florence Stirkel* thing, was good, it made me anonymous. At least, that's what I thought at first.

The work was easy. Getting safe was harder. The best way was to make myself safe from the people first, and then the school. People are always more dangerous than places.

The way I worked it out was that when I first saw someone, I'd look at their left shoulder, right shoulder, left foot, right foot. One, two, three, four; four, three, two, one. Once wasn't enough, unless it was just someone I passed on my way back and forth to school. Four times, or four times four, it had to be, for someone I'd be seeing a lot.

By the end of the first couple of days the girls in my class had started saying things when they passed me in the hall or when they sat next to me. I knew ahead of time I wasn't going to like any of them, and of course they weren't going to like me, either. I knew that the first day. Not that it mattered.

A fat girl they called Bouncer would start saying something, and then everyone would say it. "Stirkel's a Florida Cracker," or "Stirkel's a Turtle." They couldn't even rhyme right. "Stirkel" and "Turtle" don't *rhyme*. They'd be smiling their smiles so the teachers always thought they were saying something pleasant. I never said anything back. I didn't talk to them at all. I'd just stare at one of their shoulders or one of their ears, hard enough and hateful enough to grow warts on their shoulders or shrivel their ears.

Later they called me Madame Bookworm. That's because I was always reading a lot, or pretending to, anyway, just so I wouldn't have to talk to them. And it gave me somewhere to put my eyes.

All the teachers were women, except one: Mr. Flebb, the math teacher. Mr. Flebb was younger than the women teachers, and he was prettier. He had blond wavy hair and brown eyes, and he was built like a football player. At least that's what the girls said. They talked and whispered and sighed and giggled about him all the time. He'd stand up in front of the class and try to explain things and write down the formulas on the blackboard, and every time he turned his back the girls would nudge one another and sigh. He had a little cough that they thought was cute, and every time he'd raise an eyebrow, the class would melt like wax. They made up stories about Mr. Flebb and Miss Webster, the special art teacher who came in once a week. They drew big hearts saying *Mr. Flebb and Miss Webster*, and sometimes *John and Pat*. They passed notes around the class: *Mr. Flebb patted Miss Webster's shoulder and whispered in her ear when he passed her in the hall. Pass it on.*

All of this silliness filled the love-starved idea-starved idiots so full of romance they were bulging. Mr. Flebb wasn't able to teach them any math at all. But he couldn't flunk the whole class, or he'd probably be fired. So he made the assignments and the tests easier and easier and easier. It was like going backwards in time. Next we'd be adding two and two and reciting the multiplication tables. That was all right with me. Math was my worst subject.

Then one day three super-awful things happened,

all in one day, and that was a sign that there was a curse on the day or on me.

Thing one: I'd been looking at Mr. Flebb's teeth, trying to figure out whether they were real or not because they were too plus perfect, and all of a sudden my eyes jumped up to his eyes, and his eyes were looking at mine. I hadn't looked into anybody's eyes in ages, and it was like an electric shock. Eyes are very dangerous. Now he knew what I was thinking about his teeth and everything else, and he stopped smiling so I couldn't see his teeth and kept looking at my eyes, capturing them so I couldn't look away. You can see how it is with eyes, you have to be very careful. Mr. Flebb meant to get into my head.

The only place I could feel at home was the apartment. Home is where you live fifteen steps up, home is where you hang your hat, home is where you are your own private person, whoever that is, home is where you're safe from eyes that pry and probe and seek and bore.

About eyes: If you don't look at someone's eyes they can't look at yours or into yours, so they can't get themselves into your working parts, into your brain, or into your soul, or whatever that inside part of you is. Eyes: There isn't anything that can happen between people unless they let their eyes touch. It's a very useful thing to know.

Something else happened that same day, the second thing, so I knew for sure there was a curse on that day, and it wasn't over yet. Mrs. Bolton, the history teacher, a round-soft-dark, said after class: "Will Florence Stirkel please come to my office after the final bell?"

What now? I'd never said anything, I'd never done anything, I'd never looked at her, she'd never looked at me. I was an empty desk, I was invisible. I thought about how I could get sick before the last bell and spent the next couple of periods practicing. Those bells were enough to make anybody sick, anyway. They rang at the beginning of things and at the end of things and in the middle of things, trying to get inside you through your ears, trying to make you listen to them and take the sound into you, make you carry it home so you would have to keep listening to them.

I kept thinking about the bells and about being sick, but when the last bell rang I picked up my books and walked to her office. It was as if someone had wound me up and set me walking in that direction. I couldn't help it.

All the teachers' offices were in one wing of the big old drafty building. Their names were on signs that stuck out from the wall:

MISS PERKINS

MISS ATKINSON

MISS WALLINGFORD

MRS. SMITHSON

MR. FLEBB

Miss Webster didn't have an office of her own. Maybe she shared one with Mr. Flebb. I passed his office, and my eyes jumped into it, but he wasn't there.

MRS. BOLTON

Her door was open, and she was sitting at her desk. Pots of plants were all over her room and all over her windowsill and hanging all around the room. It was a regular greenhouse. I looked at her hands, which were folded fatly on the desk.

"Come in," she said heartily. "Come in, Florence." She said my name so I'd be sure she was talking to me instead of to one of the plants.

She did everything heartily, lecturing, walking down the hall, blowing her nose.

A long fern brushed my elbow as I walked in, and a hanging ivy reached tenderly towards my hair.

Mrs. Bolton was wearing a green dress. Maybe she was a plant, too, sending roots down through the floor to the basement, through the basement to the soft waiting earth below.

She brushed wisps of hair away from her face.

"Come in, Florence," she said again, her chubby arm directing me to sit in the chair on the other side of the desk.

34

I sat down, my feet on the floor, feeling them take root. Maybe all of the plants in this office were students who had been summoned in and had never been seen again. Our green uniforms gave her a head start in converting us into plants. 1905698

I sat there looking at the plants and wondering which kind I would be.

"I wanted to have a little visit with you, Florence," said Mrs. Bolton. "I wanted to ask you why you never volunteer in class. And why, when I call on you, you shake your head."

She tapped a fat finger on a file in front of her. "I have some of the papers you wrote in your Florida school, so I know what you are capable of, Florence."

She leaned forward, and I knew her fat round eyes were seeking mine, but she'd never find them. I stared at a small cactus plant on her desk. It was covered with spines: needles to prick, needles to say Stay Away.

"You're able to do much, much more than you're doing, Florence."

Why did she keep saying my name? Maybe to hypnotize me. The first step before turning me into a plant.

"Now, I know you're a new girl here, maybe shy, ill at ease because of that. A new environment, new friends, new teachers, new home ground. But I want you to do your best. I want you to start answering questions in class. I want you to live up to yourself, Florence, do your very best work here at Chilton Hall. You can do it if you will, if you want to. And I insist that each student perform to her capacity. I insist that you give me your best."

I was right. She was hypnotizing me. My eyes started to close, my head started to nod, I was being turned into the fat cactus on her desk. I rubbed my arm to see if the spines had started to come.

"As long as we understand each other, Florence," she was saying. "I expect you to complete your assignments, as always. That goes without saying. But now I expect you to make contributions in class. That will be all for now, Florence. I'll see you in class tomorrow."

I stood up, and the plants drew closer to me. My feet would not move because of the roots they'd put down. There were plants that devoured insects. Maybe there were plants that ate people. If there were, Mrs. Bolton was one of those.

Finally I pulled my feet up and away, and I was free. Free for the moment. I'd have to find a way to get out of going to history class and away from Mrs. Bolton. There was nothing, no one, who could make me stand up there in class and say something, all ears listening, all eyes watching. And that was one class I'd liked, too.

First it had been Mr. Flebb's shockful eyes seeing mine, and now it was Mrs. Bolton's prying.

Maybe later I'd have to get out of going to all of the classes. Maybe I'd have to get out of going to school altogether.

The third bad thing of the day: They said I had to have a written excuse from our family doctor if I wanted to get out of gym. Family doctor! We don't even have a family! And doctors are just for sick people anyway, and who's sick? Who wants to be? Who doesn't? Who can read a prescription blank, who wants to?

Rx plx xcuse
FI%#″ Stir′#″
fm gy#$
                    TrishgyrxMsmwe,md

Chilton Hall had been one of Aunt Nina's ideas. Just because she'd gone there and been president of the student body or something, she thought it was the only school in the world. Chilly Hall, Bleak House, Private Chill, Private Bleak, No Admittance.

My mother said Aunt Nina had even arranged for some kind of scholarship for me.

Aunt Nina this, Aunt Nina that. After going for my whole life never having heard anything about her, now I heard her name every second. All of it was Aunt Nina's fault: first our moving, then the school. And then everything, George and everything. And she was still in Europe. It was all her fault, and she wasn't even there.

THREE (EERHT)

Aunt Nina told me later that it wasn't her fault at all about George, that she didn't like him either.

But if she hadn't got my mother the job at Warwicks, my mother would never have met George in the first place.

Warwicks was a great big company that did something important. All big companies are important, just being big is important. I don't know what they do in places like that, and half the people working there never get to find out. My mother never knew.

Aunt Nina did. She had a great job there. She had to go abroad all the time, things like that. She spoke other languages and knew all kinds of things.

She'd got my mother a job because Aunt Nina knew the president and I guess almost everybody else. Not the president of the United States, just the president of Warwicks. My mother thought that it was almost the same thing.

My mother's job wasn't very important. I mean, nobody was sending *her* to London or Paris. But at least she wasn't selling seashells. I think once she was in Lattmore, Pennsylvania, my mother was ashamed of seashells. Anyway, she never talked about them. Seashells didn't seem very important at a place like Warwicks. I never did find out what they made, or did, or thought about at Warwicks. But it wasn't seashells.

We'd just had dinner, I was reading the paper, my mother was talking on the telephone. Every once in a while she'd say something, not to me, to someone on the other end. Things like, "Oh, lovely. Oh, yes. I think so, too. Perfectly delightful. Yes, I do. No, I don't." Whoever was on the other end was the conversationalist.

In Florida she never talked on the telephone. Well, she hadn't known many people in Florida. The reason she knew people here was that Aunt Nina had asked all of her friends to call my mother and invite her over. And then I guess she was meeting people at Warwicks, too.

This night when she was through with the telephone, she said that a friend of hers, a very very nice person named Mrs. Taylor, had invited me to come over after school the next day and stay for dinner. Had invited *me*.

All of a sudden I knew that Mrs. Taylor had to be Cynthia Taylor's mother. Cynthia Taylor was the dumbest, most stuck-up girl in the whole school. You can bet Cynthia hadn't invited me. She hated me, I hated her. We sat next to each other in homeroom and study hall, but she never talked to me and of course I never talked to her. She was always talking to Bouncer, who sat behind me, and their conversations were the stupidest I have ever heard, mostly about Mr. Flebb, and programs they'd seen on TV, and clothes, and hair and how many times a week they washed it.

So *her* mother had asked *my* mother. Why didn't I just say no, just spit it out, say that I wasn't going, that Cynthia Taylor had the brains of a backward chicken, that if I wanted to go somewhere or do something I'd be the decider.

I never said anything. I mean I never said anything about how I felt. I might have written it in one of my notebooks, sure, but that wasn't saying it.

Cynthia Taylor—Aihtnyc Rolyat. Miss Too-

Beautiful-for-Words. Long blond hair. Pardon *me*, golden. And she was always touching it or brushing it or looking at it. She had a little mirror in the pocket of her green jumper, and she kept taking it out and looking at it and smiling at it. I know positively she had mirrors inside the covers of her books at school so she could be admiring herself and pretending she was reading.

She was very popular at school. She looked everyone, teachers and everyone, right in the eye, just so she could see her reflection in their glasses. Every single one of the teachers at Chilton wore glasses, even Mr. Flebb.

She smiled all the time. Not just often, not just most of the time, but *all* the time. She had only one expression: sappy. Everyone kept telling her about her dimple. A dimple is a pimple turned inside out. Cynthia, Thinseea, Seeathin, Aihtnyc.

I didn't know how anyone could stand her, but she had lots of friends. All the other dumb girls with long yellow hair, like bodyguards, standing around. They looked just like her, so that even when she wasn't looking at herself, she was.

Well, so I was going to Cynthia Taylor's for dinner. Mrs. Taylor was going to pick us up after school. Cynthia hadn't said a thing to me all day, but then she never did. She kept looking over at me, though, at me or at my desk. I could feel that, so I drew a lot of pictures of dumb-looking girls with sappy smiles and long hair drooping over their eyes.

I thought maybe she'd say something after school, but she didn't, and she just grabbed her books and started outside, so I followed her. When I saw her head for a car, I knew that it was their car and that the lady driving it must be Mrs. Taylor. Sherlock Stirkel.

First I made the car safe on the outside, and then I made it safe on the inside, and then I made Mrs. Taylor safe.

Cynthia climbed in the backseat, so I did, too. All this time Mrs. Taylor was talking away. "Hello, dear, you're Florence Stirkel, aren't you? Isn't it nice that you and Cynthia are friends? Your Aunt Nina has told me all about you. Nina and I are very very good friends. She's such a lovely person, isn't she?"

She, isn't, person, lovely, a, such, she's. Then I nodded. Mrs. Taylor hardly stopped talking. "We'll be so glad to have her back in Lattmore, won't we?"

You had to be ready to nod all the time with someone like Mrs. Taylor. She kept looking in the rearview mirror at me. Cynthia was looking at her own reflection in the car window and smiling at her own smile. Mrs. Taylor kept asking herself questions out loud. "It's such a nice day, isn't it? You're a very good student, aren't you? Chilton Hall is a lovely school, isn't it? You look a lot like your Aunt Nina, don't you?"

That was a surprise.

"You and Cynthia can study together up in her room until suppertime, won't that be nice?"

If the word *nice* had never been invented, Mrs. Taylor would never have learned to talk.

I kept nodding and doing my eyes, and in a little while we were there.

I've said that I never noticed houses or buildings or streets much, and that's true. But I did notice that this big beautiful street was lined with big beautiful trees and big beautiful lawns and big beautiful houses and big beautiful cars. Even the dogs I saw were big and beautiful.

When we drove into a driveway (big beautiful), I hurried to make the (big beautiful) house safe.

First thing, we took our books up to Cynthia's room. "Now, you girls study together and have a nice visit, and I'll call you when Daddy comes home," said Mrs. Taylor.

Cynthia's room was all pink and white and ruffled and laced. There was a little heart-shaped dressing table with a heart-shaped mirror over it, and I guessed that was where Cynthia must spend all her time, admiring her smile and her dimple. There was even a pink telephone. The only thing in the whole room that wasn't pink was a green plant.

I walked around and looked around (one, two,

three, four; four, three, two, one), and Cynthia put her books down and cleared her throat and said, "What are you looking for?" There was a pink chair in one of the corners of the room, and I'd had to move it to do the corner.

"Buried treasure," I said.

"You're funny."

"You don't even know what funny is," I said. "Funny is as funny does."

"Well, you're funny, anyway," said Cynthia. "I mean about the way you act, and the way you say things sometimes."

"A lot of laughs," I said, and started laughing my hyena laugh. She started to laugh, too, after a while, because she didn't know what else to do.

"What are you laughing for?" I asked.

"Just to be polite," said Miss Perfect.

"Why am I here?" I asked. I quickly did the four corners of the pink ruffled bed and then sat on it.

"Because we invited you," said Cynthia. "Besides, your mother wanted to go out tonight and didn't want to leave you by yourself."

By myself! I was always by myself, even if my mother was right there.

I glanced over at Cynthia, but not at her eyes. She smiled at me.

Dear Aunt Molly,
I've got this terrible problem. I smile so much that

my beautiful teeth are going to catch cold. What can I do? I don't want anything to happen to them, but I do want to be sure that everyone sees them.

Miss Smile Plenty

Dear Miss Smile Plenty,
Stuff cotton in your mouth.

"You're an awfully nervous person. So you have a lot of funny habits, and that's why it's hard for you to make friends. And not having any friends makes you more nervous than ever. But I told my mother that I would be your friend," said Miss Know-It-All.

She smiled again, all dimple and teeth. I stared at her teeth.

My mother had told Mrs. Taylor that I was *nervous*. That I didn't have friends. She'd been talking about me, saying things, telling that stupid Mrs. Taylor things. What had she said? My mother didn't know anything about me, nobody did, and that's the way it was going to be forever. Nervous! What did I have to be nervous about?

A door slammed downstairs, and a man's voice called, "Fee fi fo fum, where is my honey bun?"

Cynthia started out of the room. "Guess we're going to have dinner now," she said. "And don't be

46

an old scaredy cat. Come on. You'll like my dad, he's super."

She tossed her pretty head and pushed her long hair out of her eyes. She always thought she was having a screen test. Lights, camera, action.

"Okay, Miss America," I said under my breath. I followed her down the stairs and wondered if there was some way I could trip her.

Mr. Taylor was a ho ho ho person. He gave Cynthia a big bear hug and patted me on the shoulder. "Any niece of Nina's is a niece of mine," he boomed. "Just call me Uncle John. When you know me better you can call me Uncle Johnny for short, ha ha ha."

I made him safe, and then I said, "How do you do?" (Do you do how?)

Mrs. Taylor bustled in and introduced us, told him my name, and he said, "Well, Flo, how's it go?"

At dinner Mr. Taylor kept telling himself jokes and riddles, and Mrs. Taylor kept asking herself questions.

MR. TAYLOR: What did the wall say to the floor? Meet you at the corner!

MRS. TAYLOR: Isn't it a lovely evening? John, do pass the rolls, won't you? I didn't put too much salt in the salad, did I?

That was a tricky one. You were so used to nodding that you almost nodded again.

I just love asparagus, don't you? Darling, won't it be nice to have Nina back in Lattmore again?

Mr. Taylor nodded a lot, too. I thought about the nodding turtles made of seashells and pipe cleaners and wondered if we'd all been turned into turtles and would sit around the table nodding forever.

"Why did the elephant wear pink shoes?"

But Mrs. Taylor was saying, "Doesn't she look like Nina, John?"

What were they all thinking? What had my mother told them? I tried not to do my eyes. Every time I felt I had to, I just looked down at my plate so they wouldn't notice. There wasn't going to be one single thing I would do that would make them think I was nervous. Not one single thing they could talk about afterwards.

All I could think of was getting home. If I didn't, I'd just keep nodding away until I really would turn into a turtle. Although that wouldn't be too bad. A turtle can pull in his head, hide in his shell.

I had to get away from all this closeness, three strangers, all of them watching me, waiting for me to do my eyes or something, waiting for me to look away so they could nudge one another and wink and nod.

I thought dinner would go on forever, and it did.

That's one good thing about watching television when you eat. Nobody talks to you or looks at you or thinks of you. This way it was like being in a talk show, and you knew it was your turn coming up.

Finally it was over. I went into their powder room and stared at myself in the mirror. So this is Florence Stirkel, how do you do, what funny eyes you have, hold them still a moment so I can see what color they are. Green? Blue? Do hold still, Florence. What's that on your chin? A mole? A freckle? A dimple? No, Florences don't have dimples. A pimple? A simple pimple?

I pulled my hair down over my face. There. Now no one could see me.

I waited as long as I thought I could without their breaking down the door or something. It must be time to go home, where I'd be safe. I opened the door. Mrs. Taylor was standing right outside the powder room, so she'd been spying, they were all spies.

"It's too soon to take you home, Florence. Your mother won't be back there this early."

What were they? Baby-sitters? Baby-sitting spies? Who needed them?

"I thought maybe we'd do our homework for a while, shall we?"

You notice that she had started talking teacher

talk the minute she'd suggested studying. "Let's go up to Cynthia's room and we'll study until time to go home, shall we?"

I was nodding again. So was she. Nodding was contagious around here. Then she lowered her voice and talked right. "Maybe you could look at Cynthia's English paper, Florence. I hear you're very good at spelling and grammar and everything. I'd really appreciate it if you could straighten out a few of her mistakes. I'm afraid Cynthia isn't a very good student." She laughed and shook her head, but I kept nodding. Not a very good student. That was the understatement of the century, but anyway, Mrs. Taylor was talking to me, telling me something special, just as if I was really there. Well, I'd do it for Mrs. Taylor. Not for Miss Rosebud, but for Mrs. Taylor.

Mrs. Taylor started upstairs, and I followed her. In this house people were always following people.

Cynthia was sitting at her pink desk. In front of her was her notebook. It was open, and the page was covered with splotches and blotches and botches and crossovers. Pitiful.

"We wouldn't want you to rewrite it or anything, Florence," said Mrs. Taylor. "Of course, that wouldn't be fair. But maybe you could suggest a few changes, help her with the rough spots. Spelling," said Mrs. Taylor helplessly, and she patted me on the shoulder.

She disappeared like magic, and I was left with Miss Winsome.

"You don't have to help me," said Cynthia softly.

"I know," I said. She stood up, leaving her notebook open.

"You don't even have to read it," she said.

"I know," I said again.

But I walked over to the desk and sat down. I read her paper, or tried to. If she was this dumb, you couldn't help feeling sorry for her. She would never be able to leave notes for her kids when she grew up, if she grew up. "Dinner in refrigerator, home soon," would be beyond her. Icebox? She'd spell it Eyssbocks.

Well, correcting it would be better than sitting up here in this pink ruffled and lace room staring into space until it was time to leave. I sat down at her pink desk, sighed one of my mother's sighs, and started to read her paper again.

The green plant was on the desk, and halfway through I started looking at it, and it started looking at me. After a while I could see that it wanted to be friends, so I sort of winked and smiled at it. Then I finished correcting Miss Dum-Dum's composition.

I'd kind of forgotten about her, and when I turned around she was sitting at her pink dressing table, pretending to read.

"How come your plant isn't pink?" I asked. "Everything else is."

She didn't say anything, but she walked over to see what I'd been doing.

"You didn't have to help me," she mumbled. "I could have done it."

"I know," I said.

"Well, thanks anyway," she said.

I said, she said, I said, she said, we didn't say anything. I really liked that plant of hers, and it liked me. "What's your plant's name?" I asked.

"I don't know," she said.

I could get a plant of my own. I could put it on my desk or on my windowsill. On that ledge that ran around the alcove. And I'd know its name. And it would always be there, waiting for me, when I walked into my room.

"You can have it if you want it," said Cynthia, reading my mind.

"You don't like plants," I said, reading hers.

Good, I'd take it. I had a plant, and I'd find out all about it, how to take care of it. I'd get a book about plants and what they like and need and what they don't like, but even then I'd have to watch it care-fully and tenderly to make sure it was doing all the right things. I wondered if my mother had read baby books and how-to-raise-children books. Even if she had, it wouldn't have done any good. You don't learn about people from books. At least you don't learn the things that matter, the inside deep down things. And maybe I'd never understand my new plant, no matter how much I read.

Finally, about a million hours later, it was time for me to leave, Mrs. Taylor said my mother would be home now. Mr. Taylor drove me home, and Cynthia rode along. We all sat in the front seat, all touching, it was like being in a crowded (public) bus instead of a roomy (private) car. But I held the plant on my lap and thought about it instead of about being the middle part of a sandwich.

"Cynthia will walk you up," said Mr. Taylor when we got to the apartment building, "to make sure you're home safe." Safe! "And tell your mother we'll look forward to seeing her soon."

Cynthia and I got out of the car, and she started to follow me up the stairs. The following bit again. I hate to have anyone following me.

"After you," I said.

"After me what?" asked Dum-Dum.

She really had no brains at *all*.

It was just a minute or two before my mother opened the door, but it was a very small hallway that Cynthia and I stood in while we were waiting. I couldn't be that close to anybody, not in such a small space. I did my eyes and said good night so she'd hurry and go, but she just stood there.

Then she said, "It's too bad you can't get over your funny habits. You really are an awfully nervous person, aren't you?"

"You really are an awfully dumb person, aren't you?" I said.

My mother opened the door, and we all said hello, and Cynthia finally left.

"Did you have a nice time?" my mother asked, walking around the living room, picking up magazines and putting them down again.

"Oh, sure," I said, but I didn't look at her, and she didn't look at me. I knew she didn't. I looked at my plant. Why had she told them about me? About my being nervous? I'd never forgive her, never. She'd told Mrs. Taylor, Mrs. Taylor told Cynthia. Cynthia would tell everyone at school. And it wasn't even true.

"It's so nice for you to be making friends here, isn't it?" said my mother.

She sounded just like Mrs. Taylor.

"I'm sure they'll be asking you over a lot," said my mother. "Maybe you could help Cynthia with her homework. She has a hard time with school. And things are always so easy for you."

So that was it. The Taylors would invite me over

for dinner so that I would help Miss Bird Brain with her homework. I pictured sitting at that table night after night with all of them looking at me and waiting for me to do something wrong, waiting for me to do my eyes, watching.

The telephone rang. "Oh, hello," said my mother in a special low voice that I'd never heard before. "Oh, so did I. Just loved it." Then she listened for a minute, and then she laughed. My mother *never* laughed. After a few minutes of listening and laughing, she said, "All right. See you then. Good night, George."

George. That was the first time I'd ever heard his name. My mother hung up and walked over to turn on the TV. Over the television set was a mirror. She looked in the mirror and leaned closer. She *never* looked in the mirror.

She'd been out with this George person. That's why I had been asked over to the Taylors'. That's why I'd be going over there a lot. Maybe later it would be every day. I'd be *living* over there. They'd all watch me, Mr. and Mrs. Taylor and Cynthia, and Cynthia would tell everyone at school, and if there wasn't anything to tell she'd make something up. I'd never have any privacy again. The Taylors would be trying to find out about me, trying to look into my brain, trying to pull it out a little at a time. And my mother would be out with George, thinking about him, not caring about my being stuck with Miss Awful.

I went into my room and sat down. I put the plant on my desk and started writing: AIHTNYC ROLYAT BEWARE.

Then I drew a face with long hair and jabbed it with pencil marks until I couldn't see it anymore.

I didn't write George's name or threaten him. That was to come later.

FOUR (RUOF)

The first time I saw George, I knew he was dangerous. My mother had told me that he was coming over after dinner. She was in her bedroom changing. I was looking out the living room window, watching for him. It was very important for me to see him before he came into the apartment.

A car drove up, and he got out. It had to be George. The car was between him and me. I could only see part of him, so I couldn't make him safe right from the beginning. He had those extra seconds to become powerful. I'd have to make up for it some way. Left shoulder, right shoulder, left foot, right foot wasn't going to be enough.

I tiptoed into my room. I'd have to be extremely careful. I made my room and my closet and my door and my window safe all over again. I took out my notebook and waited. I heard the doorbell and my mother answering it. Mumble mumble. Then she called me. "Florence! Do come in and meet George, dear!"

I wrote it down: raed, egroeg, teem, dna, ni, emoc, od, ecnerolf. I said it under my breath four times, using my throat and tongue and lips and Adam's apple a lot. Even my nose got into the act. Maybe that would do it.

It didn't work, of course. It was just one of about a million things I had to make up to keep George from being dangerous.

When I walked into the living room to meet him, I had to be sure I didn't look at his face. I had already decided I couldn't look at it for the first four times he came over.

I'd made every single thing in the apartment safe four times before he got there. I hoped he wouldn't stay too late, because after he left I'd have to do it again, even the steps downstairs and the outside door. I'd stopped making my mother's room safe. I never went in there anyway, and she'd have to take care of herself after this.

"So this is Florence," he was saying.

Florence, is this so.

"Well, well, how do you do, Florence?"

That was what I was waiting for, his first remark to me. Now for the hard part. Ecnerolf, od, uoy, od, woh, llew, llew.

I had to say it over to myself silently before I could answer. "Fine," I said. Enif. I could tell he was going to sit in the brown chair. I hurried to make it safe before he sat down. I didn't even care if he noticed what I was doing, if he noticed how nervous I was. The only important thing was to make him safe.

"Well, Elizabeth," he said to my mother, taking out a pipe, "what kind of day did you have?"

He was afraid to look at me or talk to me. Good.

They started to talk. Left shoulder, right shoulder, left foot, right foot, left hand, right hand, left knee, right knee, left foot, right foot. It still wasn't right. Ears. But I'd have to do his ears without looking at his face.

It was just the beginning of a long bad time. The fifth time he came I looked at his face. It was thin like the rest of him. The long thin fingers and the long narrow shoes I had seen before, of course. And the pipe. It had been very hard to make the smoke safe, because it kept moving around and changing shape.

George is a thin person, thin face, thin nose, thin

lips, thin smile, thin moustache, thin hair, thin eyebrows, thin voice, thin blood, thin ideas. He never shows his teeth when he smiles. Maybe he doesn't have any. If he does, they're really thin and sharp.

I know George a lot better now, of course. He hasn't changed a bit, except to get more boring. I have changed, but he hasn't.

He carries big lumps and clumps of silence around with him and throws one in every few minutes. This is how it went that first night. Well, and every night. His conversations are all the same, they just have different words.

You know (he says)

Lump of silence that he throws in while he's doing his pipe routine.

It's perfectly obvious

Lump of silence

That no one has written a good book

Lump

In over

Lump

Fifty years.

Bigger lump. You think he's through talking.

Not quite.

The trash

Lump

Disguised as books

Lump

Isn't fit for human consumption.
Lump, deep breath, puff on pipe
There should be a committee
Lump, and by then no one remembers what he's been talking about. You start counting the lumps.

My mother, who had never done anything at all with her hands, took up some kind of needlepoint or something. Next she'd be pasting shells together.

CONFERENCE HELD BY GEORGE LISTENERS

Friends and associates of George Hawthorne, known to his intimate enemies as Old Bore, recently held a conference to determine ways and means to keep busy while seeming to pay attention to his monologues. When asked by a reporter what subjects Mr. Hawthorne discussed, the usual answer was, "Who listens?"

My mother started seeing a lot of George, and I started seeing a lot of my room. That wasn't too bad, because I'd bought another plant and its name was Philodendron. Nordnedolihp. And I could talk to it and talk to the one Cynthia had given me. I kept them on the ledge in the alcove where they had light once in a while.

Of course, my mother was anxious for me to go over to the Taylors' so she could be with George at the apartment (to talk their private talk, I suppose?), and they couldn't go out *all* the time. And of course George was anxious to have me out of the way, too. I made him nervous. Good.

How could my mother spend all that time talking to George, when she'd never been able to say anything much to me? There *was* something the matter with me, there *was*.

This thing about the Taylors. There was no way I could sit at that dinner table again. So I said I'd go over to the Taylors' once in a while in the evening, when my mother and George were going out, if I could have dinner at home first or get a hamburger before I went. And the only way I was able to say that much was because I'd practiced with my plants for four days, rehearsing my speech. It was only two sentences, but it was a speech. My mother was too surprised to say anything. Or maybe she wasn't surprised at all. She just didn't say anything.

But that's the way it worked out. I'd eat early the nights that my mother and George were going out (or having a private time there without me?). Mrs. Taylor and Cynthia would pick me up. It would be getting dark when I left and dark when I came home, they couldn't see my face, they couldn't see my eyes.

I'd go up to Cynthia's room when I got there (following her up the stairs), and I'd give her some easy homework that was hard for her, and I'd think about my mother and George having dinner without me.

About food: Food had never been important to my mother and me. She never bothered, she never fussed, we ate to eat. Now all of a sudden she was bothering and fussing, studying recipes, trying things out, not for herself, not for me, but for His Majesty King Bore.

Why? Because she thought that he was a person and I wasn't? What else? Not that it made any difference. Nothing made any difference, least of all Georgie Porgie. Nothing was important, not food, not my mother anymore, not George, because I wasn't important. Well, my plants were important. I studied my plant book.

> Plants do not thrive if they are not wanted. If you do not care for plants, get artificial ones. They are now made so realistically that the casual observer cannot tell them from real ones without touching them.

Touch me not, forget me not.

A casual observer is someone who isn't really interested.

> Plants, like animals, go through a kind of hibernation, a dormant period when they seem to be dead. They are only resting.

Resting, resting for what?

Was I dormant, or an artificial plastic imitation true-to-life, near-to-life plant?

I don't think I'd have been able to go over to the Taylors' so often, even to get away from George, if it hadn't been for the spying. I listened to Mr. and Mrs. Taylor. And everything was terrible. Even the spying was terrible, because most of it I didn't want to hear or know about, but I couldn't help it. It was all Aunt Nina's fault, and she was still in Europe having a ball, directing traffic from a distance, pulling the puppet strings. It wasn't fair. If it hadn't been for Aunt Nina I'd have been down at the seashore, safe and quiet. Instead of being stuck with Cynthia.

About Cynthia:

> There was a young girl named Sin-thee-a
> Who was dumb as a person could be-a
> When asked why that was
> She replied "Just becuz
> My brain is the size of a pea-a."

Cynthia was too busy with her homework or too dumb to know that I was listening to her parents. I gave her lots of homework. When she wasn't working on the homework, she was talking on the pink telephone to her friends, who were calling her to find out how to do *their* homework. The dumb leading the dumb.

I'd tell her I was going to read for a while, and I'd sneak down the back stairs and sit there, and I could hear them talking.

This George Hawthorne was a cousin of Mrs. Taylor. Egroeg Enrohtwah. George was a bachelor. He had never been interested in anyone before. And now he was interested—oh, very very interested—in this Elizabeth Stirkel. No, she hadn't been divorced. She was a widow. Her husband had died years ago. And she'd never even looked at another man until now. And now she was looking at George.

Well, she had this little girl, this Florence. You know George, dear. He just doesn't know beans about children. Elizabeth wasn't too keen on his meeting the girl right at the beginning, you know how it is, dear. It might have put George off. She's bright enough, but you know, all those funny little nervous tics.

Mumble, mumble, said Mr. Taylor, and Mrs. Taylor kept talking. I didn't hear it all at once. Just a sentence here and there, some nights nothing at all, some nights a lot.

Oh, darling, you know children never say anything around adults anyway. Mumble mumble. Well, of course I've heard her talk, I'm sure I have, dear. Mumble, mumble. No, dear, she is not a mute. She isn't anything. I mean she isn't anything wrong or anything. They wouldn't take anyone like that at Chilton, anyone mental or anything. She's a very good student at school, you know. She's even got a scholarship of some kind. So in that way it's very very good for Cynthia, dear. Cynthia's never been a student. Mumble mumble. Well, of course, dear, good marks aren't everything. But they are something. And if it helps Cynthia stay at Chilton, it's worth anything. Mumble mumble. Well, of course we don't have to adopt the poor little thing, you always exaggerate so.

Yes, George has met her and everything. And it's all right now because George is head over heels.

Mumble mumble, said Mr. Taylor.

Well, of course, darling, we all know he's not a head-over-heels *person*. But wouldn't it be nice. Nina's sister-in-law and our George.

That was one night they had to take me home early because I had this awful headache. Or stomachache. Anyway, they had to take me home early.

Mumble mumble.

I was quiet as a plant is quiet, drinking in their words as a plant absorbs water, letting the words fill me—sending my roots out to gather every drop, pulling every ounce of nourishment from what they were saying, filling myself, glutting myself on the words.

And they kept coming, too many words, and maybe my searching roots would rot, but I could not shut them out now. It was too late. The more I heard the more I wanted to hear.

Mumble mumble.

At the office. She met him at the office. She works, you know. I guess her husband didn't leave her a penny.

Mumble mumble.

No, of course she's not after George's money, dear. She's a very very nice person. And George doesn't have any money. Or at least he never *spends* any.

Mumble mumble.

They didn't need to act as if I was some freak or something. It was true what Cynthia had said that first night: nervous people get into the habit of doing some dumb thing over and over. Everybody does something sometime to ward off an evil spirit or an approaching scare or storm or a bad experience or maybe an old memory that tries to come back—fear of the past, fear of the future.

There was a little boy at the school in Florida who

always touched all the posts of the fence at recess. He never had time to play any of the games. He'd run around desperately touching each post. It was a big enclosed playground, so it took a long time. I watched after school to see if he did it then, too, and he did, and then I watched early in the morning, and he was almost late because he had to touch the posts first.

And there was a girl who wouldn't step on cracks, and a funny kid with adenoids who started every sentence by saying yeah, ho, yeah, and a fat boy named J. C. who blinked his eyes and squinched his nose all day long.

Maybe it had started by accident. Maybe J. C. was really upset or worried or anxious or afraid about something when he was a little kid. Maybe he thought somebody was going to hit him, or maybe he thought he was going to wet his pants. Anyway, maybe he happened to blink his eyes and wrinkle his nose, and the bad thing didn't happen. So maybe without even realizing it himself, he just went into that routine every time he was nervous, every time he felt threatened, and that's how it started, maybe, and maybe not. I don't know, because nobody knows what's going on inside of anybody else's head, or even inside their own head.

Knock wood, appease the gods.

Maybe J. C. didn't know why he was doing it,

but he knew he had to keep on doing it. He couldn't stop. If he stopped, who knows what would have happened to him?

And who knows what would have happened to me if I'd stopped doing my eyes?

Maybe we were all strange, the little boy who touched the posts, the girl who wouldn't step on cracks, the kid who said yeah, ho, yeah, J.C., me: strange, funny, different, odd.

Mumble mumble.

They didn't always talk about me.

Mumble mumble.

Yes, Barb and Joe are coming over for bridge tonight. Now don't say a word about his hair, dear. It always gets the evening off to a poor start. He's so sensitive about getting bald, and he doesn't think your jokes about it are a bit funny.

Mumble mumble mumble mumble.

Mrs. Taylor laughed.

That one *is* funny, now. I wonder if I'd dare tell Barb.

Mumble mumble.

No, I don't picture George as a father, either. Maybe they'll just send her away to camp or school or something.

I pointed my two index fingers in their direction. Bang, you're dead.

I stood up and tiptoed back upstairs to Cynthia's

pink and white room. I stood outside her door and listened. She was talking on the telephone. Maybe she was talking about me. I opened the door and walked in. She was brushing her hair with one hand, and holding the telephone with the other, and smiling into the heart-shaped mirror. She didn't see me right away, but she jumped when she did. She's such a scaredy cat.

FIVE (EVIF)

George started coming over for dinner almost every night. They weren't going out as much, and I heard Mrs. Taylor telling Mr. Taylor it was to save money.

I'd eat in my room, carry it on a tray. My mother was getting to be a pretty good cook, now that she was interested. I said I had a lot of homework to do, and that was true. I had a million papers to write and a million tests to study for, because I was trying to skip a grade. My mother was glad I was studying and glad I guess that I was eating in my room. It made her nervous to have George and me at the table at the same time. I made my mother nervous, I made George nervous, I made myself nervous.

About studying: Studying and getting good grades wasn't hard for me, because that's all I really had to do or wanted to do. And thinking about it was important, because it kept me from thinking about anything else. If I was figuring out an algebra problem or writing an essay on the Industrial Revolution, there wasn't room in my brain for anything else. So I'd spend all the time I could on homework. When I ran out of homework, I'd make some up. I'd write new endings to books I'd read, or I'd make up a new character to go in a book to see if he or she would or *could* possibly change the plot.

The best way for me to do homework was while I was watching TV. That way, if I stopped thinking about algebra or history or whatever, there was something going on on TV, something to put my eyes on, something to get my ears to do, anything to keep from thinking about what I didn't want to think about. Now that George was here, I couldn't watch TV while I studied, so I had to study more and more and more. And now I had my plants to take care of, transplant, divide, watch over. I'd bought some new ones.

About your brain: Every single thing you've ever seen or heard or felt or learned or done is in there, it's all waiting to be remembered. Some things are on the main highways of your brain, some are on little back roads, and some are on dark paths in the woods, with tangles and brambles. But they're all there, all those memories, all stored in there. Nothing fades, nothing disappears. It's all there waiting, waiting to be discovered again, waiting for you to trip over it once more.

You have to ride fast on the highways so you won't have time for the woods.

One night when George and my mother were having coffee in the kitchen, I went into my closet to look for some old notebooks that were way at the back.

And I heard George talking, just as if he was talking right into my ear. Then I realized that the breakfast nook must be right on the other side of my very long closet. I'd never pictured it that way before. If I had, I'd have been in there from the beginning, listening. I was getting very good at listening.

I held very still.

GEORGE: . . . wrong with her?

MY MOTHER: Oh, nothing, George. She's just a little nervous. She's a very high-strung child. She's doing very well in school, that will be good for her, working hard. She always gets good marks. I'm sure she's going to be fine.

GEORGE: . . . always like this?

MY MOTHER: Oh, no, not for a long time. When her father died, she did develop these tics, but she's been fine until we moved here, then she seemed to start them all over again. Change is hard for her. And of course it got worse when you and I—

GEORGE: You mean I'm a change?

MY MOTHER: Well, in a way, of course, George.

GEORGE: I see.

MY MOTHER: Now don't have hurt feelings. You're a nice change for me. But it's hard for Florence. We've been very close, you know, we've had only each other for a long time.

Close! If that was close, what was far?

MY MOTHER: But she'll get used to it. She just needs a little time.

GEORGE: She seems very odd. What's the matter with her eyes?

MY MOTHER: I told you, she's just nervous. She'll get over it. It's just nerves, just tics.

After all, she's just a child. Children
outgrow things. It's nothing for us to
be worried about.

Us—she said *us*. And odd—he said *odd*.

GEORGE: I hope not. Speaking of worries
(lump), I heard today that Steffins
(lump) is going to get the ax.

MY MOTHER: Steffins. Oh, that man in your de-
partment.

They started talking about the company. I waited
for a long time. Then I went back to my desk. I drew
a picture of George smoking his pipe, and then I
drew more and more smoke until you couldn't see
George anymore, just the smoke, and he was chok-
ing to death under the smoke.

EGROEG ENROHTWAH YOU WILL DIE

After that I listened every night. George did almost all the talking. There were about a million
pauses, what with his eating and his swallowing and
his pipe and his boringness.

GEORGE HAWTHORNE WINS TROPHY

George Hawthorne, Executive Associate of
Warwick Associates, today won the Blue Rib-
bon Talk Trophy, outtalking and outboring

many contenders. When asked about his reaction to this triumph, George Hawthorne was so nonplussed that he could hardly talk, and his acceptance speech lasted less than three hours.

He talked and talked. And I waited and waited. He'd be talking about me again. Sure enough.

"She's doing it on purpose," said George.

"Oh, George, she's not doing it just to annoy you, dear," said my mother. "It really isn't anything to get upset about. It's just water, after all."

"It's annoying and (lump) it's wasteful (lump). Be sure to speak to her about it."

So he'd noticed. That was going to make it harder.

I heard George go into the living room, and in a minute I heard my mother going in, too. I waited until I heard George's voice from the living room. Mumble, mumble, lump. Mumble, mumble, lump.

Then I crept across the hall to the bathroom. I turned the faucets on, very carefully, very slowly, all of them. The ones in the washbowl, the ones in the tub. A drop at a time. It had to be just right. Then I went into the kitchen and did those. When I came back to my room, I took out my notebook. I drew George's long narrow face and his thin hair and his eyes inside his glasses. BEWARE EGROEG

ENROHTWAH. I stabbed it with pencil marks until I couldn't see it anymore.

It took a long time to make my room safe that night. I shifted the plants around in the alcove until I felt a little inside click, a sigh that meant they were arranged just right, friends next to friends.

. . . Did you say anything to her about the water dripping? Always *her*, or *she*, never my name. He was afraid to say my name, because that would make me powerful.

All my mother had said to me was, "Be sure to turn the faucets off tight, Florence." Did she know? Did she think I was just careless, or did she know? I'd keep on doing it anyway, of course. I had to.

On my way out of the closet that night I'd seen that old doll lying on the shelf where I'd left it. I carried it into my room and put it on the chair. For decoration.

I kept listening, and I kept studying. I studied a lot so I could get out of that grade and into the next one. Maybe if I really studied, I could finish school right away, be through with Chilton Hall and Mr. Flebb's eyes and Mrs. Bolton's nosiness, and George, and get out of Lattmore forever, go back to an ocean, the ocean, my ocean, back where everything was the way it used to be. But it could never be the same again, it was all over.

I tried to crowd my brain full of things. And

Cynthia's head. Cynthia didn't have a brain. I listened to her parents when I was there, and to George and my mother when I was home.

I filled two notebooks with my newspaper articles and pictures of George. And I still had time for my homework, and Cynthia's, and my plants. I had a lot of plants now.

Plants. I knocked a plant out of a pot to transplant it the way it said in my book about plants, and I saw its exposed roots twining around and around, nowhere to go, like all the nerve ends in my brain, all matted together. I was all roots, no green, my nerve ends twining, falling, climbing, sprawling, spilling, winding, crawling, reaching back on themselves inside my skull.

SOCIAL NOTES:

Miss Florence Stirkel, Lattmore's most popular hostess, today entertained a select group of friends in her charming penthouse, decorated handsomely with wet sphagnum moss. After exchanging ideas and making plans for future get-togethers, the guests were served a delicious repast of H_2O seasoned with fish emulsion and bone meal. Included among the many guests were Mmes. *Plectranthus australis, Schlumbergera bridgesii, Saint Paulia jonantha, Euphorbia splendens,* and *Campanula isophylla alba.*

I learned a lot from my how-to book, everything except how you shouldn't look at a plant's roots, it's too private, too personal, too violating, the plant shrivels and dies if it's exposed to eyes, but this plant book didn't know that.

There are lots of books to tell you: Too much water and the roots will rot, the plant will die, too little water and they'll dry up, too much sun, too little sun, too much cold, too much heat, cool, shade, dry, warm, medium light, high humidity, there are books to tell you. But there is no book to tell me about myself, *Florencia erratica*, avoid overcrowding, do not expose to bright lights or to eyes, keep cool, avoid transplanting, be careful of thorns.

Thorns: If I were really a plant, I could have thorns, like a rose, or prickles, like a thistle, or spines, like a cactus, or poison, like a nettle.

As it is, I don't even have *finger*nails. I bite them.

I would have to depend on thought waves, hate waves, waves to shrivel George up. If we looked into each other's eyes, which of us would wither and die? Or would it be like the Gingham Dog and the Calico Cat, we'd eat each other up?

I listened, and still George never said my name. That showed he was afraid.

My mother always used my name, whether she was talking to me or about me. She referred to me by name to remind herself that I existed.

Even plants have nicknames: busy lizzie, prayer plant, wandering jew, spider plant, mother-in-law's tongue, waffle plant, toad lily.

Toad lily. Turtle Stirkel.

I practiced sending evil messages to George, and finally my witchcraft worked. My hate waves and my drawings of him had done it. Good.

He had to go away. He had to visit his parents in Oregon. Imagine George having parents. George, Egroeg, egghead, eggplant, plant an egg and up comes George.

Maybe my mother and I would go back to our old routine, having TV dinners together and watching the programs and maybe talking at the commercials, and maybe talking instead of watching anything at all. Or maybe it was already too late for that because of George and because of knowing things were going to change. If you know things are going to change, it's as bad as having them change right then. Worse. Anyway, we never had a chance to see what would have happened if we were by ourselves, because Aunt Nina came back.

Of course I'd known she'd be coming.

COMING!

Nina Stirkel!

Sister-in-law of Elizabeth!

Sister of James!

Friend of the Taylors!

Executive of Warwicks International!

World traveler!

And!

Last and least!

Aunt of Florence Stirkel.

I was in my room, studying, or writing things for my newspaper or doing my plants or just staring, I don't know. My mother had washed her hair and was drying it while she watched TV.

The doorbell rang. I heard my mother walk over to answer it, and then I heard a couple of happy shrieks and then some other sound and then laughing. My mother was laughing, and someone else was, too. As I've said, my mother almost never laughed.

In a minute I heard someone running down the

hall, and someone burst into my room. I didn't even have time to make her safe. She threw her arms around me and hugged me. Then she pulled me out of my room and down the hall to the living room.

My mother was sitting on the couch, still laughing.

"Oh, Nina," she said. Aunt Nina was laughing, too. She didn't let go of my hand. She'd put a big pillow under her coat, and when my mother had answered the door, she'd thought Aunt Nina was pregnant. That's why they were laughing. That, and being glad to see each other.

"Why didn't you tell me you were coming?" asked my mother. "Here I am, my hair's wet, I'm a mess, the apartment isn't even picked up."

"I wanted to surprise you," said Aunt Nina. "Besides, I wasn't sure when my plane was getting in, and I didn't want you fussing or thinking you'd have to meet me or anything."

"Florence and I have eaten, but I'll fix you something," said my mother.

"I'll fix something," said Aunt Nina. "Spaghetti with chocolate sauce, how's that sound, Florencia? Pizza with strawberry jam?"

She didn't wait for an answer, she turned back to my mother and started laughing again. "Remember how he used to order a pickle sandwich with gravy? The waitress would think he was joking. But he'd convince her, and when she brought it he'd really eat it, and like it. Pretend to, anyway. Remember the time—"

I hadn't looked at her face yet. I'd count to a hundred backwards, and then I could look.

"What about you, hon?" asked Aunt Nina, turning to me. I was only as far as forty-nine, but I looked at her face anyway.

"You've eaten, but how about some dessert? Mashed potato sandwich?"

I didn't answer, but maybe I smiled, or maybe her smiling at me made me think I was smiling too.

She had short curly black hair and black eyebrows, her eyes were green, she was very pretty, but you didn't notice that so much, you noticed the way she moved. All the time her face kept changing. It didn't settle down to one expression for more than a few seconds. She was smiling, laughing, frowning, looking surprised, or excited, or delighted, or something, all the time. My mother's face has only about two expressions. Aunt Nina's face was never the same twice in a row. I watched her that night the way I'd watch a special television program.

Not just her face and eyes moved, her hands and arms and shoulders and body moved, she acted everything out while she talked, she never sat still. It was as if an extra person inside was spilling out, spilling over. She made everything and everyone else seem sluggish, slow moving. Especially my mother, and George, and me. We were all sleep-walkers swimming through sand, and she was the only one alive.

She wanted to see the whole apartment. "I've bought some more furniture," my mother explained. "It's pretty empty, the way it is."

"Perfect for dancing," said Aunt Nina, whirling around, grabbing me and spinning me around and around until we were dizzy. I wasn't used to being touched, my mother never touched me. And here was Aunt Nina, grabbing my hand, that first second, and she'd given me a hug in the living room, and now she was spinning me around, involving me, bringing me into her orbit so that I felt somehow connected to her.

While we were showing Aunt Nina the apartment, my mother noticed the faucets dripping in the kitchen and in the bathroom. She didn't say anything, but she turned them all off, tight. I'd have to fix them later.

Aunt Nina insisted that I stay with her in the kitchen. Not just to be polite. She wanted me there, she really did, I could tell. But why? Why would she want me around, why would anyone? No one had before.

Out of odds and ends in the refrigerator she fixed

a snack, and then my mother came out to the kitchen, too. Watching Aunt Nina was like watching a play. She acted out some of her adventures in Europe. She imitated everyone who had been near her on the plane on the way back, she made even her ride over to our apartment in the taxi sound exciting and dramatic. Was she making it all up to entertain us, or did everything happen? Was everyone's life that much fun, *could* everyone's life be that much fun? Was it just the way she looked at things?

Afterwards, we sat in the living room, the three of us—the *three* of us, I, Florence, not only included, *invited!* They talked, I listened.

Nina was telling a story about one Easter Sunday in New York, how she and Jamey rented a wheelchair for the weekend, when they were kids, and took turns pushing each other up and down Fifth Avenue for the Easter Parade. Everyone coming out of church would see Jamey in the wheelchair, and when enough people were seeing him, glancing at him sideways, Jamey would say, "Wait, wait, Nina—I think I can walk! Yes, look, Nina, I can, I can walk, it's a miracle!"

No one was really fooled, but they smiled. Nina and Jamey took turns pushing each other. Suddenly I realized that she was talking about James, my father. James Stirkel, Jamey, Nina's brother, my mother's husband, my father.

"Yes," said my mother, "James loved things like that, playing games, fooling around."

Nina started to laugh again. "Remember when he used to—"

Jamey, Jamey, Jamey. I'd never heard anything about him before tonight.

My mother didn't mention George, not once, not all evening.

Aunt Nina came over again the next night and fixed dinner, something simple, something delicious, different, foreign. And the night after that my mother and I went over to Aunt Nina's apartment, at the other end of Lattmore.

"Welcome," she said, opening the door with a flourish. She wore a turban and dangling earrings and a long sleek dramatic dress. "Forgive my elegance. I absolutely had to do something to dazzle. It's the exotic side of me that I'm trying to cultivate."

Her apartment was modern and bright and beautiful: brilliant paintings on the walls, figurines and masks from other times, other worlds; books on shelves, magazines piled everywhere, her apartment was alive as ours had never been and could never be.

There was a fireplace, the fire leapt and crackled, the sound and smell and sight of its warmth as important as the warmth itself.

Everything in her apartment had a story, a story

about the way she came to have it, an encounter with a strange old man in a flea market, a curious message left at her hotel, a gift from a fish peddler, a painting she'd bought when she was in Paris with Jamey, they'd bought it together from a sidewalk artist who had come to be their best friend, who had come to be famous.

Jamey again, and tonight I heard more and more about him, the fun they'd had, the games they'd played. How he'd stand with Aunt Nina on a busy street corner and point up. "It was right there, I swear it," he would say.

"Oh, don't be silly," she'd answer. "There isn't such a thing as a flying horse."

And then she'd look up and gasp, "I see it, I see it!" and they'd stare up, and soon a lot of people were staring up, too.

I tried to picture my mother having a light-hearted, funny, nonsense time, and I couldn't.

And still no mention of George.

Aunt Nina said, "We've all been invited to the Taylors' for dinner tomorrow night. Florencia, I hear you and Cynthia are friends."

Friends? Hardly. But what's a friend, who's a friend? Maybe I'd never have a friend, maybe a friend would never have me.

Aunt Nina went on. "I'm so glad, she needs a bright friend. She's been so self-conscious about being slow that I'm afraid she always chose girls who weren't terribly bright, so you'll be good for her. Poor love, she's been in those braces since she had teeth."

"What braces?" I asked.

"You'd have to have noticed. Dear heaven, even her braces have braces, and rubber bands, and hinges, and miscellaneous metal devices."

"She doesn't have braces anymore," I said.

"Well, that's a blessing," said Aunt Nina. "She was always afraid to smile. I'll be glad to see how she looks now. She was always a plain child. Very very sweet, but very very plain. Limp hair, muddy skin, and of course all the braces." She looked over at me. "You're so lucky, hon, to have been pretty right from the word go."

Pretty! I did my eyes.

"Well, and bright. Cynthia's always had such a hard time in school. She's such a dear, a very thoughtful and nice girl, but she needs someone like you around, someone who's interested in things."

Were we talking about me, Florence? And Cynthia? Miss Dimple?

So Miss Swan had been an ugly duckling. Maybe I'd have liked her better if I'd met her then. It's a lot easier to like someone homely than someone beautiful.

I tried to imagine the plain Cynthia but I

couldn't. Well, anyway, the improvements were all on the outside. Too bad they couldn't straighten out her brain while they were doing her teeth.

I guess I always think of people the way they are now, not the way they used to be, or the way they might be. Just the way they are now, this year, this month, this week, this day, this hour, this minute. I couldn't even remember how my mother had been before she'd met George, when she and I would go to the beach together and watch TV and know each other's days.

We all went to the Taylors' the next night. This was my social season. Anything was fine, even the Taylors', everything was fun when Aunt Nina was around.

Mr. Taylor was very whimsical. "A rose between two thorns," he said, sitting on the couch between Aunt Nina and my mother. "An island totally inundated by waves and waves of beautiful women."

"If only George were back," said Mrs. Taylor, smiling and nodding at my mother. "You'd be two islands."

"Yep, share the wealth." Mr. Taylor smiled.

"I'd forgotten to ask about your cousin George," said Aunt Nina. "How is he?"

There was a little quick chat about George for a minute and that was the last of that. There wasn't really too much you could *say* about George. Aunt

Nina didn't know about George and my mother, then.

Everyone was in great spirits that night. Cynthia told some stories about school that were funny, Mr. Taylor told some of his jokes, and Aunt Nina told us some more stories about Jamey. About my father, James. She acted it all out as if we were playing charades.

When Cynthia and I had gone up to her pink and white rosebud of a room to get my coat, she said, "I never even thought about you having a father. He must have been a fun guy."

"Sure," I said.

"It's too bad he died," said Stupid. "Mom said it was years ago. What did he die of when he was so young?"

"Old age," I said.

"I bet you hardly remember him," said Cynthia.

That night I waited awake until my mother had gone to bed, and then I did all the faucets. And I made an invisible line all around my room. I got out my notebook and drew Cynthia and wrote SHUT UP AIHTNYC ROLYAT.

Who was it who had sat on my bed and told me stories and played me games and said *Sleep tight, Birdie?* Who was it who loved me so and called me Birdie?

SIX (XIS)

I had a seed
and forgot to plant it
I had a friend
and forgot to smile
I had a song
and forgot to sing it
and so I walked, and so I walked,
and so I walked, for many a mile

I forgot to tell about that. Miss Perkins had asked
us to write a poem. That one was mine. It's pretty

sappy, but you should have heard the others. Anyway, old Perkins really loved it.

"It shows the real you, dear," she had whispered to me. Which was pretty silly, of course. Just because you write something, it doesn't mean you feel it. Just the opposite. If you really feel something, you can't write it at all.

Anyway, after the poems were turned in, she read them all out loud. One thing good, she didn't tell whose was whose. Then she decided to use mine as a kind of class exercise. "You know, class," she beamed, "I had a hummmmm and forgot to hummmmm it."

The things that class came up with must have made old Perkins wince, but she kept smiling and nodding and calling on the next girl. I had a car and forgot to drive it. I had a shoe and forgot to tie it. I had a fish and forgot to feed it. I had an egg and forgot to eat it.

There was this really pretty girl in that class—Holly—beautiful big brown eyes and, you guessed, long golden hair. A really mean girl, and when Miss Perkins called on her, she said, "I had some hair and forgot to comb it."

The reason this was mean is that Perkins never did comb her hair. Every Monday after school she'd go to the beauty parlor and get it done. Then she'd put on a net and sleep in it, I guess, and Tuesday morning you could see the mark the net had made on her forehead. Her hair was all waved and curled and sprayed and everything, and except for the net marks, she didn't look too terrible. Then the next day and every day all week it got to look more and more slept on, and finally it looked as if it had been glued together in bunches. You can picture Monday, before the beauty parlor. Anyway, it was mean of Holly, and mean of everyone to laugh, but Perkins just called on the next girl.

There was this little dark girl in class—Punchy they called her—all jump and muscle and bounce. And she kept putting her hand up and Miss Perkins kept calling on her. Her contributions were things like: I had a stone and forgot to throw it. I had a nose and forgot to pick it. I had a bath and forgot to take it, things like that, and Perkins never batted an eye. Maybe she wasn't even listening. She'd just nod and smile and look around for another hand.

I had a joke and forgot to tell it, I had a dream and forgot to do it.

Cynthia's was: I had a test and forgot to get an A on it.

One thing about Perkins, she never laughed mean, I'll say that for her. She was always saying things to make you feel better. It never made *me* feel better, knowing the source, but it was nice anyway.

I see I said . . . *nice anyway*. Nice! But it was.

Something good was in the air, some extra sparkful thing, like Christmas, but it wasn't Christmas. Excitement, secrets, surprises danced invisibly around me. Even Cynthia seemed to be more like a regular person, less like a doll, more like maybe a friend in the making, a could-be friend if I'd stop trying not to be one. Maybe it was because I knew about her braces and knew too that she'd been plain and so could forgive her dumbness, or maybe I was just getting used to her. Everything seemed better.

It had started one night by the fireplace, at Aunt Nina's. She had asked us over, but my mother wanted to stay home to defrost the refrigerator. Isn't that sad? Something else sad: She never learned how to defrost herself. Is there a little dial someone could turn?

Anyway, I was glad it was going to be just Aunt Nina and me. Someone would be talking just to me.

"I have a theory about fireplaces, sunsets, and far places," said Aunt Nina while we were watching the fire after supper. "They warm your soul. Expand it. Strengthen it. Ready it for the supreme adventure, the great lovely mysterious voyage."

I wasn't sure I knew what she was talking about, but she was talking to me, not at me, not around me, not calling hollowly from the very long distance of adult to grown child, the very long distance for example from my mother to me, Florence.

"Just fireplaces, sunsets, and far places?" I asked.

"Just for starters," she answered. "They're the first on my list right now. And friends."

"You're not going away again to another far place?" I asked, suddenly uneasy, suddenly frightened.

"Oh, no, because I have a fireplace here. And a new friend: you. Besides, I hate to pack suitcases. I'm always forgetting something."

Packing a suitcase, forgetting something—there was something here, some sudden memory, but I stepped quickly over it, left in there in the tangles and brambles.

"Jamey and I used to roast marshmallows in the fireplace at home," she said. "Next time I'll have some here, and we'll do that."

"You had fun," I said. "You *have* fun."

"Always." Aunt Nina smiled.

"I wonder what my mother would have been like if she'd been raised the way you were," I said.

"It isn't the way you're raised," said Aunt Nina. "It's the way you are. It's the way you want to be that matters."

I thought about that for a while, sitting there looking into the fire. The way you want to be? Could you choose, really choose? Or were you programmed from the word go, acting out a part because you were assigned to it, it to you? Did I have a choice—could I be like my mother or could I be like Nina or could I be someone else entirely, a grown-up Florence? A grown-up isn't just an older version of a kid, it's a different person altogether, isn't it? Is it?

The fireplace night (that first one, there were many) was the beginning of the best time, the beautiful time. It didn't last long, that blissful easy time, but while it was happening, I thought it might last forever. Whatever is happening I think will last forever, especially if it's something happening inside me. Or is that where everything happens?

Was it Aunt Nina who had made all the difference? Or was it because Georgie Porgie was gone? Or was it because the roots in my brain were getting straightened out (because I was growing taller?), finding somewhere to reach, new things, people, places, ideas? Maybe it was the stars.

I was a Pisces and I always read my horoscope every night in the newspaper, but I never read one thing I believed. How could the stars have anything to do with anything? Why? Why not?

One of the things I started to study when I was running out of interesting things to study at Chilly Hall was vineyards.

About stars and grapes, grapes and wine, stars and people, grapes and people: There are good places, good vineyards to grow grapes, grapes for wine, but the place isn't everything, the soil isn't, not the whole answer, not the whole scene. It's the sun and the wet and the cold and the hot, the cool and the warm, and the wind and the stillness and the time of all these in relation to one another, and also the this and the that, things no one knows about, the meanness going on in the neighboring village, maybe, nobody really knows. They keep records, they've kept records for ages, but they still don't know for sure ahead of time whether any year will be great or mediocre or terrible or anywhere or everywhere in between.

That's the way it must be with people, the placing of the stars, the planets, the sun, the wind, the clouds, the this, the that, at the moment of your birth, combined with the place of your birth, the vibes at the time, and all that combined with your own genes and chromosomes and molecules and inner root system. Don't forget that, you stargazers with your charts, out there gazing out instead of in here gazing in! Maybe you can tell something about me by looking at the stars, but what about looking into me through my eyes into my brain, heart, soul, etc. (Etc.: Nickname of etcetera, aretecte, an escape hatch. You can always say etcetera if you don't want to figure out what all you really mean. *E.g.: I am nervous, strange, etc.*)

But this was a good time, sparkful, as I said, something in the peculiar combination of wind and weather and wet and dry and the inner tickings and tockings of one Florence Stirkel.

Just as I'd decided I didn't need anybody, not

anybody, not even my mother, whom I'd always needed before, along came Aunt Nina. Did I need her because I liked her, or because she liked me, or was it all the same?

Do plants love the sun, or does the sun love plants? No matter; suddenly someone with a green thumb had carried me up from the basement and put me on a windowsill. I could feel the difference, suddenly I knew everything would be all right, I could put out new shoots, send down new roots, grow to be whatever it was that I was going to be, and I could hardly wait to find out.

What a delicious chunk of time that was! Going over to spend the night at Aunt Nina's, sleeping on the couch in the living room that folded/unfolded into a bed, watching the fire after she had gone to bed, the rise, the fall, the in, the out, the pull, the push, the up, the down. . . . It was the closest thing I've ever known to being next to the ocean.

HOUSEHOLD HINTS

INGREDIENTS: fire, air, water, earth, sun, love
DIRECTIONS: mix in equal proportions
              and wait
              wait and see

Mrs. Bolton, Cynthia, Mr. Flebb, George, Jamey, my mother, Nina, in alphabetical order, all mushed together, all diffused in the low hushering of the fire, the sharp corners soft now, everything was going to be all right, I was going to be all right, that was the first time I'd ever believed it. I used to take my notebook over to Aunt Nina's and write in it there:

> I fall asleep
> when the fire is eating the logs
> and when I am awake again
> the logs have eaten the fire!

Used to. I said *used* to, but I wonder how many times I went. How many days, weeks, months, how much time are we talking about?

About time: Something happens, something good, something bad, but something happens, and because of the goodness of it or the badness you think about it over and over. So later you don't know if you are remembering many *times* or just the many *memories* of a time or two. . . .

Because this is still winter, same year, same place, same station, so how long was I happy? Two weeks, three? Forever, never?

One night when Aunt Nina was over, my mother said, "George Hawthorne is coming back to town. He's taking me out tomorrow night for dinner. I thought maybe you and Florence would like to have dinner here. That way you could see him again for a minute. I know he'd love to see you."

Aunt Nina was rearranging some flowers she'd

brought over that night. She turned and looked at my mother. "George Hawthorne—he's a friend of yours?"

My mother nodded. "A very good friend," she said. She must have been embarrassed, admitting that. I'd be embarrassed if I had a friend like George. And of course the reason she hadn't said anything about George before was because she must have known Aunt Nina didn't like George.

"George Hawthorne?" asked Aunt Nina. "George B. Hawthorne, B for Boring? Elizabeth, he's a stuffed owl."

My mother smiled her sweetest smile. "Nina, you may form your judgments, I can form mine. I've never criticized Alan, and you must know how I feel about that relationship."

"That's over with Alan. It's been over for a year. It just didn't work. But it was good because he's a good man," said Aunt Nina.

Then they both remembered I was in the room and they didn't say anything else about George or Alan, whoever he was.

George was back. I guess my mother was glad to see him. She called me in from the bedroom to say hello, just like that first time. I never had learned a way to make him safe, and I never would.

"Well, well," he said. "Well, well (lump). How's it going?"

I supposed the first thing he'd do would be to check the faucets. He'd find them dripping, if he did. I was glad they were going out for dinner.

Aunt Nina came just as they were leaving. Aunt Nina and George were very polite. It was, "How have you been, George?" and "It's good to see you again, Nina," but you could tell my mother was glad to leave with George.

Aunt Nina and I had our stew in the kitchen. "Do you like George Hawthorne?" asked Aunt Nina.

She was so different from my mother. My mother would never have asked me anything like that about anybody. She never asked if I liked someone or how I felt or anything. She never has, she never will.

"Oh, sure," I said. I hadn't learned when to tell the truth and when not to. I still haven't.

"I don't," said Aunt Nina. "He's a very pompous, very boring man." She smiled and shook her head. "I shouldn't say that. He's solid. Substantial. Someone you can lean on if you feel like leaning. And I guess your mother feels like leaning."

I didn't say anything.

"Maybe it's been lonely for her," said Aunt Nina.

I'd never thought of that. Why would she be lonely?

"Remember, hon, no one's all good. No one's all bad, either. Everybody's a little of this, a little of that." She sighed and looked at her stew. "I love stew," she said. "I don't like the carrots, but I like the stew, and as long as the carrots are there I'll take them along with everything else. Your mother may not like George's boringness, but she likes George. She takes the boringness along with him."

I didn't say anything. I was thinking that I wished my mother would talk to me the way Aunt Nina always did. I ate my stew and thought about what Aunt Nina had said. I didn't like my mother's silence, or her liking George, but I liked my mother.

Ever since then carrots have reminded me of George's boringness.

A couple of nights later my mother invited Aunt Nina and George over for dinner. "Try to like George, Nina," my mother said. "You will if you want to. He's a wonderful, solid, kind man. You can't judge him until you know him better."

I know Aunt Nina was thinking the same thing I was—you have to get to know him before you can really hate him.

We all ate together in the dining room, because Aunt Nina insisted on it. George and my mother wouldn't want me, they never did, they never would.

Aunt Nina and I had set the table. "Let's do place cards, to make it seem like a party. And we can make funny hats," she said. "Jazz things up a little. We'll need it, believe me."

I made the place cards while she made the hats. I drew pictures of all of us instead of writing our names: a kind cartoon of George and his pipe, Nina in an airplane, my mother stirring a huge bubbling pot on the stove, me reading, what else?

And we made up funny fortunes for everyone and folded them small and put them in tiny nut cups.

George thought it was all very foolish. He wouldn't wear his funny hat, and my mother finally took hers off, to show that she was on his side, I guess. She didn't want him to think he was the only poor sport at the party. She read him his fortune: "Look, George, isn't this cute? They've made fortunes for us. Here's yours, listen." Couldn't George *read?*

After dinner, Aunt Nina said, "Elizabeth, why don't you and George go on in and visit, and we'll bring your coffee in, won't we, Florencia?"

When we were in the kitchen alone together, she whispered, "Next party we have, we'll plan the guest list."

We took in the tray with coffee and the tiny thin cookies she'd brought over. I wasn't going in, but she said, "Stay with me, you have to, for moral support. I can't handle George alone."

So I went in and sat. I wouldn't have to say anything. Saying anything at all around George was a physical impossibility for me, like swallowing my nose or something. I was just there. I brought in a pad to doodle on and a book just in case. I hated to just sit and listen, unless I was in my closet or on the Taylors' kitchen steps. It's easier to listen if no one can see you. Aunt Nina started leafing through a magazine. With George around you couldn't really concentrate on anything. You always had to be ready to listen to him. And he didn't like to have other conversations going unless they were his kind of conversation. The only time you could really talk when he was around was when he went to the bathroom. And of course when he did go, he'd notice the faucets.

I didn't know how much Aunt Nina already knew about George and his Georgeness. He was starting his pipe routine, so for the moment he wasn't talking. You'd think it would be all right for someone else to say something, right? Nina did. "Elizabeth, you remember Liz McAfee. She's had her hair cut short and streaked, and it's taken years away, she looks really beautiful."

George cleared his throat. A signal, but Aunt Nina didn't know that. She kept talking. Of course, my mother knew George. So she said, "Nina, I think George was going to say something."

Honestly.

Aunt Nina looked over at George and smiled politely and dangerously. He cleared his throat again. A speech.

"The wasted energy (lump) that goes into the cosmetic industry (lump) is absolutely incredible. Do you realize (lump) that the average American woman (lump) spends more on cosmetics (lump) than she does on shoes?"

"Where did you hear that?" asked Aunt Nina.

"Common knowledge," said George, lighting his pipe.

Aunt Nina didn't say anything for a minute. She kept leafing through her magazine. My mother was ready to listen to George again. She always was. He was still fussing with his pipe.

"Well, speaking of cosmetics, here's a new idea," said Aunt Nina, stopping at a page. "All the big companies are coming out with it next season. It's colored enamel for the teeth. Sort of like nail polish. Colors to match every costume, every mood. Colors for your teeth coordinated with your nails and hair and eye makeup."

She paused. "I'm just wondering about my new little black suit, the one I bought in Paris. I suppose I could have *contrasting* teeth. Black's so outré, don't you think? I mean for teeth. Gray might be nice with the black, or maybe a pretty lavender. What do you think, Elizabeth?"

I was looking at Aunt Nina, and she looked up at me before I could look away. She winked.

"Really, Nina," said my mother.

"Really, Elizabeth," said Aunt Nina. "I think I missed my calling. I could have been another Elizabeth Arden or Helena Rubenstein. I'd love to invent cosmetics."

George was about to say something.

"I really think it's a great idea," said Aunt Nina. "On the Fourth of July, everyone could paint their teeth red, white, and blue."

I doodled and drew George. He was feeling threatened by Aunt Nina, so he made his lumps fewer and farther between.

Sample conversation:

GEORGE: This women's lib. Ridiculous. It's just a fad (lump). There are only a few women who want things changed (lump). They're just a bunch of (lump) frustrated spinsters.

AUNT NINA: You know, you're absolutely right, George. If God had felt that men and women were equal, he'd have made the sky half blue and half pink.

MY MOTHER: Oh, really, Nina.

I started to draw my mother. I never had, before. I drew her with two faces, one looking right, one looking left. Which way was she going to go?

SAMPLE GEORGE REMARK:	Television is terrible. All of it (lump). There isn't a single program worth watching.
MY MOTHER:	The news is interesting, George. The news programs.
GEORGE:	Slanted. It's all slanted (lump). There's nothing you can trust. All the commentators are Communists. Television is terrible. Mark my words, there isn't one decent program.
AUNT NINA:	Yes, George is right. If God had wanted us to have television, he'd have had Noah put two in the Ark.
MY MOTHER:	Oh, Nina, don't tease George. George, she's only teasing.

George left early that night, because I was sending him bad vibrations, and of course Aunt Nina was, too.

After that I'd go over to Aunt Nina's when George was coming for dinner, and sometimes Aunt

Nina and I would go to the Taylors'. How often? Two times, a thousand times?

George got sick, he had another cold, he always babied himself, went to bed with the sniffles, and Aunt Nina came over a lot that week. She was teaching my mother a lot of recipes so she could surprise George.

One night I was in my room, doing my plants, wondering why there had been so much electricity in the air that night at dinner. I went into the closet to listen. My mother and Aunt Nina were finishing something in the kitchen. Then they made coffee and sat in the breakfast nook where I could hear them.

". . . serious about George Hawthorne, Elizabeth."

"Why not? Why can't I have my own life, for a change?"

"Your own life is one thing. George is another. You'd never be yourself with George. El Boro."

"I never criticized Alan."

"You never knew Alan."

A long silence. I held my breath. Had they heard me?

Aunt Nina's voice. "How could you possibly be interested in George after Jamey?"

"You think James was the only person in the world, that's why," said my mother. "He wasn't perfect, believe me."

"I wasn't saying he was perfect, I was saying . . . "

"I'm sick of hearing about him," said my mother, but it wasn't my mother's voice. "Jamey this, Jamey that! He was just another human being. You've made him an idol, no faults. Games, games, games! That's all you and Jamey ever thought about! There are other things! Bills! Responsibilities! Growing up! James never grew up!"

"He never had a chance," said Aunt Nina.

"I was married to him, not you," said my mother. "The big charmer, the great big beautiful little boy! Well, you can't laugh your way through life, Nina."

"You can try," said Aunt Nina.

"At whose expense?" asked my mother. "George isn't a bundle of laughs, but he's got a head on his shoulders. He's kind and considerate. He'll take care of me. And he loves me."

"Jamey loved you," said Aunt Nina.

"In his way! And I loved him! But that was then! He's dead, he's gone, I can't carry him around inside me the way you can! I can't make the old days come back again! I can't and I don't want to! The wheel-chair thing. How many times did I hear it? How many times did he tell it? Both of you, a couple of kids in never-never land! You think he was perfect. You keep looking for someone like Jamey, some-body perfect. Well, nobody's perfect, Nina. Not George, not James, not Alan, not anyone. And I'm not waiting my life away, not anymore! I'm not pretending that somebody or something in the past was better than I remember!"

Was this my mother's voice?

"All right, all right," said Aunt Nina. "Don't shout. We sound like a scene in a soap opera."

They did. It was a scene. I see a scene, I've seen a scene, a scene I saw, I saw a scene, the scene was seen. Except that I was only hearing it. A radio soap opera.

"Sorry," said my mother.

"I wouldn't want Florence to hear us," said Aunt Nina.

"She can't hear us, she's at the other end of the apartment."

A long silence. Were they listening for me?

Then my mother: "I didn't mean to say anything against James. Or Alan, either. Did I say anything against Alan?"

"No, that's all right," said Aunt Nina. "I'll try not to say anything more about George. I just want you to be happy."

"I want to be happy, too," said my mother.

Was she staring at Nina, into space, into her coffee cup, was she crying?

I said everything had been good, had been special, but something went wrong, something turned sour, something in the air, something in the stars, something in the wind, the fire went out. It was Aunt Nina's fault. Or was it mine? Or was it the stars rearranging themselves and thus rearranging me?

Aunt Nina suddenly announced one night when she was over for dinner that she was going back to England for a visit. England! What for? What about me? I felt as if someone had dropped me in an ice bucket. I didn't say anything at all, I couldn't, and later when she said, "Hey, hon, I'll miss you, hope you miss me, too," I said something like, "I'll try to manage," I don't remember, something sarcastic anyway, and she put her hand over mine.

"A rose has thorns for its enemies, not for its friends," she said.

"The only reason you like me is because I'm half him," I thought, whispered, said, cried, called, shouted, dreamed.

"The only reason I like you is that you're all you. Nobody is half of anybody. And if you were half Jamey, if you could be, you wouldn't be feeling so sorry for yourself!"

Her anger was a quick flash of lightning, and it was over in that bright instant that it began: the words echoed blazingly in my head like a road sign of some kind, a signal, a warning, a direction.

Sorry for myself?

"Look, hon, it's too bad about George and your mother, I agree, he is a drag. I know how it is, you're so intense, you're bound to take things hard, but it isn't the end of the world."

She didn't even understand me! I didn't care about my mother and George, not anymore. I cared about Aunt Nina. She'd made everything bearable, everything possible, made *me* bearable, made *me* possible, and now she was going, throwing me back to myself.

And saying that it wasn't the end of the world! It was, it *was* the end of the world because it was back to life as usual, back to me as usual, this is where the program starts all over again: nowhere, nothing, no one. It was very much the end of the world.

I went to my room early, I tried to write something in my notebook.

What now?

Now what?

was all I could think of to write. I got ready for bed, but I knew I'd never be able to go to sleep. I went into the closet to listen.

". . . more time, I don't know."

"What about Florence, if you marry George?" As if she really cared. She didn't, she couldn't. Not if she was leaving. She didn't have to go, she wanted to. She'd said a visit, not a business trip. A visit.

". . . I've thought about it," said my mother. "And

of course George and I have talked about it quite a bit."

Discussing me with George, helping him to get inside me so he could direct the intricate traffic.

". . . think she should be busier? Friends, activities. And maybe you could spend more time with her, don't give her time to brood."

"Oh, Nina, Florence is very busy. She likes to be alone, she's very independent."

Likes to be alone, loner, lonest, unconnected, unconnectable, no ties, no gives, no takes, the solo person, soloing into space.

"I'm going in to say good-bye," said Aunt Nina.

I hurried out of the closet and jumped into bed. In a moment Aunt Nina knocked at the door.

"You all right, hon?" she asked, coming over.

All right, all wrong.

"Sure," I said. She sat down on the edge of my bed. It reminded me of something—what? My mother had never sat on my bed, she had never tucked me in. What was it that was so familiar, like an old melody trying to come back and live with me and haunt me and drive me and devil me? What was it I could feel but not feel, a shadow?

"I wanted to say good-bye," said Aunt Nina.

"Good-bye," I said.

"I'll be back," she said, leaning over to kiss me good-bye. When she straightened, she was smiling.

"Jamey always used to say, 'I'll be back when I'm back, sooner than soon, but not today, alackaday.' " I didn't say anything, but my heart pounded.

As soon as she had left the room, I sat up in bed. "Don't go!" I shouted soundlessly. "Don't go away! If you leave me, I won't love you."

Something had turned from shadow to substance, from dream to hard, something I'd been hiding from, running from. I got up and made my room safe as soon as I heard Aunt Nina leaving the apartment. Then I made the closet safe all over again, and I went back to bed. Something was trying to get into my head, no, it was already there, had been there always, was waiting.

As soon as my mother was in bed, I got up and did all the faucets. One drop at a time, one drop at a time. Not too slowly, or they'd get separated. If the faucets were turned off tight, that waiting drop would get caught up there and the rest wouldn't wait for it. They'd be separated forever, and it would be my fault.

I walked around my room, I lay on my bed. With my eyes closed, trying to see inside my head, with my eyes open, trying not to see.

"Come help me pack, Birdie, you can put a kiss in my suitcase for good luck. Put it right on the top, next to the hankies." He picked me up and put me on the bed next to his suitcase. "Should I take two shoes or one? One sock or two? Someday I'll take you along, Birdie, sling you over my back like a little papoose or smuggle you in under my coat. What's that you've got there, sir? A little girl, I do declare, sir! And at a business meeting, come come!" He closed the suitcase, and carried me in to my own bed.

"Here's a going-away present from me to you, Birdie. Listen." He whistled. "Anyone else hearing it won't know what it means, because they'll only hear its outside, they won't hear what it says on the inside. It says *I Love You Birdie*. Now listen again."

How did it go—a little tune—I Love You Birdie —da *da* da dada? Twee *lee* de leelee?

"Did you put the kiss in my suitcase for good luck?" I nodded. "Then I'm off. I'll be back when I'm back, sooner than soon, but not today, alack-a day. 'Bye, little muffin."

I sat up in bed. "Don't go!" I called. "Don't go away! If you leave me, I won't love you."

. . . The good luck kiss. Now I jumped out of bed. I'd made my room safe and everything in it safe, but something was wrong. Of course. I'd made everything safe but myself. How could I have forgotten that? I remembered now the way I used to do it, the way I made myself safe, long ago. Wink left eye, right eye, jerk left shoulder, right shoulder, left foot, right foot. Move move tap tap. Something more . . . left foot, then knee, then shoulder, elbow, wrist, each finger, back up the arm to the shoulder, move left side of face, wink left eye, then right eye, move right side of face and so forth on down to my right foot, right toes. . . . I did it four times, then four times four, I could do it all the time if I had to.

"I'll be back when I'm back . . ."

SEVEN (NEVES)

I had to keep thinking of new ways to make everything safe and safer. If only Aunt Nina hadn't gone back to Europe again. It didn't matter, she'd left, so she didn't care, no one did, not now, not ever.

George was coming over almost every night. And I always listened, there at the back of the closet, making myself safe over and over again.

. . . our life together, Elizabeth.

. . . am thinking about it, George.

. . . again.

. . . be fine, don't worry about it.

. . . looked into a fine school while I was in Oregon (lump), boarding school (lump), great staff (lump), specializes in problem children.

. . . not a problem, George, not really. I told you. She's just nervous. She'll outgrow these little tics, wait and see.

. . . time. Psychiatrists are all quacks (lump), but a splendid school, a school geared for these difficult youngsters (lump), disturbed.

. . . not disturbed. I don't want to send her away.

. . . have to recognize, Elizabeth.

I wouldn't go over to see the Taylors. Cynthia kept calling me, and my mother kept worrying at me about it, but I couldn't go, I didn't want to see them, I didn't want to see anyone, I didn't want to go to school. I pretended I was sick so much that I *was* sick. I felt like a plant that everybody had forgotten to water, I kept putting my roots down farther and farther, but it was all sand and gravel and grit. I was all alone on a dark desert, or maybe an abandoned windowsill, in a clay pot, no escape.

GALLANT GIRL NEAR DEATH'S DOOR

Florence Stirkel, victim of a rare disease, has been deluged by cards from well-wishers all over the world. "Tell them all thank you and . . ." She smiled bravely at this reporter and swallowed. "And good-bye."

I did get one card from Cynthia, and one from Miss Perkins.

I missed a lot of school, and I didn't even want to read. I just practiced being sick all the time. It was pretty boring after a while, and when I got really bored, I got better. And I spent a lot of time on my plants, transplanting them and trying to plant new shoots to make new plants.

While I was sick, I found new things to do to make my room safe. It took a long time every day. One thing: I drew invisible powerful lines all around it, like cord wound tight. I began noticing that the room was getting smaller. If it got too small, I could crawl out the window. But what about the plants?

There wasn't anyone to talk to. When would Aunt Nina come back? If only my mother had been like Aunt Nina, or if George had been like Jamey, or if Cynthia had been like Miranda. I hadn't thought about Miranda for a long long time. She had been my best friend. We could always talk about anything and everything. Miranda was always the same. She never changed. And she was always interested, interested in *me*.

It was funny that I'd been thinking of Miranda, because when I walked into my room that day, she was sitting there waiting for me. It was as if we'd never been separated. And I was right, she hadn't changed, she'd never change, any more than Jamey would change.

When I saw her, I hurried in and shut my door. Then I told her everything. About Aunt Nina, and about how she'd gone away again, and about George and my mother, and about George wanting to send me away. "And I'm not going," I told Miranda. "It's some school for oddballs. I'm not going off to some new place like that. I couldn't ever get it safe. I've made it safe here."

"Let's run away," said Miranda.

"Where would we run?" I asked. "There isn't anywhere, there isn't anyone."

It was true. There wasn't anyone. There was Aunt Nina, yes, but she was gone.

"Remember the way we used to run?" asked Miranda. "We'd take a little suitcase and a little lunch—peanut butter sandwiches and an orange—and we'd tiptoe out and . . ."

"That was then!" I said. "We're too old for that now!"

"Remember when they'd find you, remember she'd be so nice, and afterwards you wouldn't have to do anything different or go anywhere different or anything?"

I remembered.

"Let's go," said Miranda. "There's bread and peanut butter, and I saw some apples and bananas on the kitchen table."

I hesitated. Aunt Nina wouldn't have liked this, wouldn't have liked it at all, but she was gone, and Miranda reminded me of that. "If she'd cared, she'd be here," she said. "It's so easy, let's go. You know they'll find us right away. But not too soon. They'll have a chance to get really worried, especially your mother, and she'll blame George. It's his fault, really. And then you'll never have to leave this safe place."

Miranda was right, she'd always been right, she'd always been my best friend, she'd always cared about what happened to me. Aunt Nina didn't care anymore, but Miranda did.

We got everything together, and we started to run down the apartment steps.

Someone was coming up. It was Aunt Nina. It gave me a terrible jolt to see her.

"Hey," she said, "I'm back!"

I just stood there.

"Where are you going with that suitcase?" she asked. "And that doll?"

I didn't know what she was talking about for a minute. Then I looked down. I was holding a doll. I was holding my old doll, Miranda.

"Let's go up and make some popcorn," said Aunt

Nina. "I haven't had popcorn in ages. I've missed it. And I've missed you a lot, hon."

My mother was still at work, she'd be coming back pretty soon now. I didn't want to listen to Aunt Nina, I could tell she knew something was wrong, and I knew if we started to talk she might push me into those dark tangled woods I'd been trying to stay away from.

I made her safe and ran down the steps to make the front door safe and the newel post, and then the stairs on the way up and the railing, and all the time I was making myself safe, too, so that I wouldn't have to remember anything.

I carried Miranda into my room and put her back on the chair. Aunt Nina came in. Right eye, right cheek, right side of mouth, neck, right shoulder—

She put her hands on my shoulders.

"Hey, hon, what's wrong?"

"It was my fault," I said, saying it out loud for the first time, remembering it for the first time in a long long time as I said it, remembering that it was my fault but still forgetting what I had done.

"What was your fault, hon?"

Yes, what? I listened to my voice, wondering what it would say.

"That he died," I heard myself whisper.

And suddenly the remembered dreadful frightened lonely times of long ago closed in, and I was hating myself, fearing myself, shocked into numbness by his dying and by my guilt, my hidden unspoken unspeakable unforgivable secret.

"What do you mean?" asked Aunt Nina. "It was no one's fault."

The good luck kiss, the one he wanted me to put in the suitcase. I hadn't put it in at all. I was angry and hurt because he was going away, leaving me again.

I'd nodded when he asked me, I'd lied, he thought the good luck kiss was with him, he thought he was safe. He went away and never came back.

"I was mad at him," I said slowly.

Aunt Nina put her arms around me.

"I can't remember the whistle," I cried, and we rocked back and forth.

I fell asleep on the living room couch with Aunt Nina sitting beside me. I was sleeping when my mother came home; dozing and dreaming and drifting. I heard them talking, I lay there on the couch, my roots stretching silently and smilingly towards the words, towards the love that was in the room, that was in the world, waiting, and that I now drew into me to grow on.

THE END (DNE EHT)

Well, George and my mother got married and sent me off to this school. Of course it isn't the kind of school that *George* had in mind. Aunt Nina wouldn't have put up with that for a minute. My mother would put up with anything, if she'd put up with George.

I brought along a cactus, and it put out a flower last month, can you believe it? At first I hoped that was a sign: something significant, something meaningful, but later the cactus died, along with the flower, so now I hope it didn't mean a thing. Probably I watered it when I shouldn't have or didn't water it when I should have, or maybe I breathed too much on it or at it or too little, or maybe gave it too much shade or too much sun. I'll never know what I did wrong or what it did wrong, or maybe it died because its time had run out, it wasn't my fault.

One night long later I told Aunt Nina about the good luck kiss and she hugged me. We talked about it, we talked about me. Why had I been nervous for so long? Why did I have all those tics? Was it the good luck kiss? Maybe; and maybe not. If it hadn't been that, it might have been something else that happened or didn't happen. Maybe the combination of stars and sunspots and vibrations from growing things under the ground and growing things inside me said: Worry, Florence Stirkel.

I don't know and Aunt Nina doesn't know and nobody knows. Maybe it's just rough edges getting smoothed, or smooth edges getting sharpened, maybe it's just growing up.

George took my mother to Frankfurt, Germany, for their honeymoon. If they had a baby they could call it Hotdog, I told Aunt Nina. We were sitting beside her living dying fire.

"Weinie Hawthorne," she said. She looked over at me. "You could be Florence Hawthorne if you wanted. Hawthorne's a pretty name."

"I'll stick with Stirkel," I said.

"OK, stuck with Stirkel," said Aunt Nina, "until you get married."

She poked the fire, and it blazed and later faded.

Honestly, if I thought I'd end up marrying someone like George, I'd rather die.

"Aunt Nina, why didn't you ever get married?" I asked one time, just after my mother and George went away. I was staying with Aunt Nina, I stayed there all summer.

"Never say never," laughed Aunt Nina. "It's like playing cards. Draw, play, discard. I've just had lousy cards."

"George is such a pill," I said. "I can't stand having him for a stepfather. Kids should be able to have a say."

"Nonsense," said Aunt Nina. "You can't choose your stepfather any more than you can choose your father. It's your mother's life, so it's her choice. And you're going to be growing up, anyway, so it really won't make that much difference to you. But it will to her. Your life is coming up now, and then you can make your decisions, just the way she's making hers now. You can understand that." She smiled at me.

Well, I understood it. You can understand something without liking it, and I told her that.

I've grown up more or less, less or more. But I couldn't have done it without Aunt Nina.

"Without someone," she corrected me, when I told her that. "There are lots of people around, billions, you just have to put yourself in the way of getting to know them. You won't want to be everybody's friend, but you've got to learn how to start."

Well, that's right. You have to have a friend to be one. I even got to be friends, sort of, with Cynthia. She wasn't all that bright, but she was *nice*. Aunt Nina said it was a good jumping-off place.

And now that I realize that the world is full of Aunt Ninas in different shapes, sizes, disguises, life seems pretty exciting. It isn't all Georges, by a long shot.

This school isn't too bad, if you like boarding schools, which I don't. It's not all good, of course, but what is? Nothing's perfect, no one, I've learned that. But nothing's all bad *either*. There are a couple of nice teachers—get that word, nice—and I'm in an honors program, and I've decided I'm going to be an English teacher, how do you like that? I guess if I could teach Cynthia anything, I can teach anybody.

And I went to a dance last week and met a boy from another school, and he said I was interesting. Interesting!

So I'm here and waiting, and as Aunt Nina said, I'll be growing up anyway. Anyway up growing. Up growing anyway. Growing anyway up.

ABOUT THE AUTHOR

Florence Parry Heide is the author of many popular books for young people, among them *The Shrinking of Treeborn*. Her first novel, *When the Sad One Comes to Stay*, was published by Lippincott. Her collaborators include her daughter Roxanne, with whom she is working on a series of mysteries for young readers, and composer Sylvia Van Clief, with whom she published over a hundred songs.

Mrs. Heide grew up in Pittsburgh, where her mother, Florence Fisher Parry, wrote a daily column for the *Pittsburgh Press*. A graduate of UCLA, Mrs. Heide now lives in Kenosha, Wisconsin, with her husband, attorney Donald Heide. The Heides have three sons, two daughters, a daughter-in-law, and a son-in-law.